Regrets *and* Promises

Dennis McGarry

printed by

Petoskey, Michigan

Regrets and Promises

ISBN 0-9764133-0-2

First Edition Printing
December 2004

 All the events and characters found within these pages are fictional and exist only in the mind of the author. Any resemblance to any person, either living or not, is purely coincidental.

Cover concept and design by Kim Whitley

For Stacy
the one true love of my life

David,

It takes five days to travel from Venice Beach, California to Trufant, Michigan on a Greyhound bus.

I don't recommend the ride.

I stepped off the bus in Trufant just after midnight in late July of 1974 with a battered suitcase in one hand and a brown paper bag in the other. The drugstore/bus stop in front of me was closed and dark except for a single globed lamp suspended above the door. Stepping into this dim pool of light, I turned and looked up and down the main drag of the little town as the angry diesel fumes from the departing bus settled around me.

There wasn't much to see.

Setting my bags down on the sidewalk, I sat down on the curb with my feet in the gutter and fished out the crumpled pack of Kools I had managed to stretch out over the last seven states and two days.

The old man had given me a five-dollar bill and the one and only hug I ever remember getting from him just before I got on the bus in California.

"I know it's not much," he said with a shrug and a bleary-eyed smile, "but that's all I have left."

At the time I thought he was talking about the money so I thanked him and told him it was enough, I'd be fine. Looking back now I'm more inclined to think he was talking about the hug. Either way my answer would have been the same.

I spent the last forty cents of my five dollars on that

pack of Kools when the bus stopped for fuel just outside of Boulder, Colorado. I had a good pack a day habit going at the time and was more worried about going without cigarettes than food. Everything I ate after leaving Colorado was on the five finger discount plan; Sardines, Vienna Sausages, Spam, if I could open it without a can opener and if the can would fit in the top of my sock under my pant leg (thank God bell bottoms were in style), it was lunch. I never stole candy bars or potato chips or anything else I might enjoy eating. I had it figured out that getting caught stealing canned goods that a guy wouldn't eat unless he were really hungry would be a lot less apt to earn a call to the local law than, say a pack of smokes or a candy bar.

I shook out one of the last two cigarettes left in the pack and lit up. Crossing my legs in the gutter, I smoked my cigarette and went back to looking my new hometown over.

Three streetlights spaced about a hundred feet apart bathed the whole town in deep shadowed light. Across the street from me a small, secure looking bank stood next to an even smaller, less secure looking post office. Two tidy looking houses filled out the block.

My side of the road held a Zepher gas station on the far corner, a grocery store (or 'food mart', according to the painted wooden sign hanging out over the sidewalk) and the drugstore I was sitting in front of. A dirt parking lot between the grocery and drugstore completed the town.

"Oh, this is going to suck," I moaned to myself.

Now I was no stranger to moving. Before my folks got divorced the old man had always done his best to get four or five months of living out of any apartment we had rented for the two months rent he had to pay to get us moved in. Dad always seemed to know just how far he could push any landlord unfortunate enough to rent to the Malone's and he pushed every one of them right to the breaking point before moving us out in the dead of night while all the respectful, rent paying tenants in the building were sleeping. So, like I said, moving wasn't a big thing for me.

Moving to a small little town out in the middle of nowhere, on the other hand, was a very big thing. I was a born and raised city boy and had never lived in any city that didn't encompass at least four separate zip codes. Most of the buildings I had lived in were bigger than this whole town, for God's sake, and a lot of them were seven or eight stories tall!

And the noise... there wasn't any noise in this open empty space that called itself a town. No sirens, no cars, no neighbors fighting or crying or laughing. How could anyone fall asleep at night with no rhythm of traffic or footsteps in hallways?

There were more houses in the town of course. I could see the occasional front porch light winking through the trees and bushes for a block or two behind the buildings across the street and I assumed there were more behind my side of the block as well- but there still couldn't have been more than a hundred people in the whole town. I felt like I had just landed in the middle of a Twilight Zone episode where, for the first time in my life, I couldn't see another living person and there was no one to see me.

I was fourteen years old and had never felt so alone.

Taking one last pull off my smoke, I flicked the butt out into the street and reached back for my suitcase. Snapping open the buckle that still worked, I rummaged through the thirty-odd paperbacks inside before deciding on a Louis L'Amour western that I had only read two or three times since I had stolen it from the Carnegie Library back in Venice Beach. Old Louis was never one to dilly dally with a story and within a minute or two I had vicariously cheated a hangman's noose with the help of an old Indian woman and her son and was riding off alone through dust devils and shimmering heat waves toward the safety of the blue mountains far off in the distance. My body was still sitting on a lonely sidewalk in a strange little town but the empty feeling in the pit of my stomach was gone and my mind was two thousand miles and a hundred years away.

I have a whole slew of memories from when I was a little kid but two of them have always been a matched set of misery for me that have never seen fit to visit one without the other.

The first, like all my memories from childhood, is your standard issue black and white reel that lasts about ten seconds. This particular clip features an overweight Detroit cop knocking on the door of the apartment my mom and I had been living in since my parent's divorce eight months earlier. I looked up at the cop after opening the door and saw he had what looked like a dab of yellow mustard on the underside of his chin. The cop looked down at me and asked if my mom or dad was home. As the cop talked to me, I noticed the mustard was caught in a double chin wrinkle on his fat face and was actually squishing back and forth, making a very soft, lubricated 'pop' sound as he talked. I smiled a little bit at how gross and disgusting this was (thirteen-year-old boys really enjoy shit like that) while telling the cop that my mom was working downstairs in the bar. The cop took a deep breath and told me that he was sorry but the woman working downstairs had been stabbed to death. The cop went on to say some more stuff but I was having some trouble hearing him over the growing sound of that mustard drop squishing in and out of his double chin fat. I looked away from the cop's face and tried to ignore the sound but it kept getting louder and meatier with every syllable that fell out of his mouth until finely I couldn't even hear the sympathetic voice of the cop anymore over the wet, sloppy squishing sound of that damned yellow mustard and I had to scream at him, "WIPE IT OFF! WIPE IT OFF! WIPE IT OFF!" until everything went dark.

Second billing on this double feature of personal anguish is a bit older and longer but just as clear and sharp as the first.

It was Saturday morning and I was sitting cross-legged on the floor about two feet away from our thirteen inch black and white TV. I was still in my p.j.'s and watching The Rocky and Bullwinkle Show, my favorite cartoon in the whole world.

"Hey, Rocky," Bullwinkle bellowed. "Watch me pull a rabbit out of my hat."

"Again?" Rocky and I replied in skeptical unison.

"Well, here's the little slut now."

My dad's whiskey-smoothed voice burred from the easy chair he had passed out in hours earlier while waiting for my sister to get home. I heard the apartment door close behind me and turned my head from the TV to see Cindy standing in the doorway looking pale and scared. I couldn't see the old man. His chair, which had always faced the television, had been turned sometime in the night to face the apartment door. I heard a kitchen match pop and flair and slender tendrils of smoke floated up around the tan vinyl.

"Daddy, I..." Cindy started, taking a step forward.

"Nothing up my sleeve," Bullwinkle announced, his moosey voice followed by the expected ripping sound.

"Get out." The old man's voice knocked my sister back against the door with the finality of the two words. There was a movement in the hall off the living room and I saw my mom standing there holding an overloaded laundry basket of dirty clothes. She had her coat on for the walk to the washing machines over in the next building. The coat was threadbare and shabby.

"GrrrRRRrrrrr!" the animal that Bullwinkle had

pulled from his hat roared from the tinny speaker of the flickering box behind me.

"I might have married a whore but I'll be damned if I'm going to raise one." The old man's matter-of-fact, quiet voice hit Cindy and found its mark. Her left arm wrapped itself across her wounded body as her right hand scrabbled over the surface of the door behind her, blindly searching for the knob. She moaned and I started to cry.

"No doubt about it, I gotta get me a new hat," Bullwinkle finished.

Cindy found the doorknob and stumbled out into the hall, leaving the door open. The old man stood up and walked across the floor to the doorway. Putting his cigarette in his mouth, he deliberately closed the door softly and snapped the deadbolt home. I looked over to the hall entrance and saw the dropped laundry basket spilling the last of its dirty clothes out onto the floor. A door to one of the three bedrooms off the hall slammed.

I quickly turned my head back toward the TV to avoid meeting my dad's eyes and cried silently while Sherman and Mr. Peabody chatted amicably about Christopher Columbus. I wouldn't realize I had wet myself until halfway through the next cartoon.

Cindy never even tried to come back after leaving that morning; she might as well have died that day for all I heard about her over the next few years and I worried about her constantly. I remember asking my mom about her once after the two of us had left the old man and moved on to Detroit, but mom just started to cry and said she didn't know.

After mom died I was shipped back to California to live with the old man and his new, younger wife, Sheila; a bleached blond, thirty-year old bar fly with big boobs and a proportionately small brain. Sheila lived under the impression that the old man was thirty-two and didn't have any kids. The old man clued me in on this little charade when he picked me up at the bus station after mom's funeral.

"Your mom was my mom too, you got it?" he said, steering the car with one hand while fishing a pint of Jack out from under his seat with the other. "You call me Leo from here on out or I'll break your arm." Unscrewing the cap from the whiskey, he poured a healthy slug into the empty pop can between his legs, recapped it, and slid the bottle back home under his seat.

"You always were a smart ass," he said, tilting the can at me and giving me a wink, "but at least you know how to watch your mouth. You won't forget." He took a long pull from his pop can and swallowed with just a hint of a grimace. I turned and stared out the window of my dad's car feeling homesick.

I fell right into my role as the invisible little brother at the old man's apartment and things went along okay for a lot longer than I ever expected. The fact that I was probably clinically depressed over mom's death helped, of course (I could hardly bring myself to do anything other than show up at school during the day and read books from the school library in my bedroom at night), but you didn't have to spend much time around Sheila to know that the sun and moon had better revolve around what she wanted and I knew having her Romeo's little brother underfoot every day wasn't going to last.

At first I was impressed at how hard the old man worked at keeping his new young bride happy. Impressed and more than a little pissed off. It seemed to me that if he had only put half of the effort into keeping the same job, the same apartment, and paying the bills on time back when mom was around as he was for this ditzy bitch, mom might have stuck it out; she'd be alive and life would have been just fine.

I guess I started to hate the old man there for awhile until I started to notice little chinks appearing here and there in his armor of good intentions - a call from a bill collector one day, going into work an hour late the next, calling in sick one day a week after that - and it finally occurred to me that the old man hadn't changed a bit. He was just putting on a show for his new wife... only now the new Mrs. Malone wasn't quite so new anymore. Once I got that figured out, I knew it was just a matter of time before Sheila found herself sleeping next to the same man my mom had married.

The honeymoon came to an end five months after I moved in. The old man got fired and went on a three day drunk. After he sobered up he got another job driving a cab out of the airport, but being the newest driver meant working the overnight runs for about half the money he had been bringing in from the factory. Sheila had to go back to being a bar waitress, bill collectors started calling more and more often until the phone company finally cut off our service, and Sheila's car, a sexy red Mustang Mach One she had bought before she married the old man, was repossessed.

I could see the handwriting on the wall and it scared me. I went out and got a job delivering newspapers to pay for my own food and cigarettes but there wasn't any way I could disappear altogether and I could tell that the old man and Sheila were seeing dollars going straight down the toilet every time they looked at me. I started wondering what it would be like to live with foster parents or in an orphanage.

My moving papers finally came through one morning in the form of a bus ticket propped up in front of a cereal bowl on the kitchen table. I read the ticket over while I ate my Captain Crunch, packed what little I had to take with me and waited for the old man to get home from work. The ticket said my bus was leaving at eleven that same morning. The destination was listed as Trufant, Michigan.

Mom and I had moved to Michigan because that was where her parents lived and she thought it would better to live closer to them than the old man (and I'll never understand how she ever came up with that idea. Her folks didn't care about her anymore than dad did, especially after they found out she wasn't there to repent and join their 'One True Church') but they had lived in a subdivision of Detroit called Royal Oak. Detroit was a big place but I was pretty sure I had never heard of any town or subdivision called Trufant. The one thing I was sure of was Michigan got awfully damned cold and snowy in the winter and I wasn't too wild about that.

The old man made it home half drunk with just enough time to get me across town to the bus stop.

"You want to guess who you are going to go live with?" he asked magnanimously, looking over at me with drunkenly sly eyes. I shook my head as I watched the light above the intersection we were blowing through change from yellow to red.

"You," he announced, pointing at me with a shaky index finger, "are going to live with Cindy."

I looked over at the old man in surprise.

"That's right," he smiled and nodded, looking back to the road. "I figured you'd like to go see her again so I arranged the whole thing. And it wasn't easy either, let me tell you." The old man paused and glanced over at me to see if he still had an audience. "No, sir. I went to a lot of trouble to find your sister and work this all out. I could see things weren't working out for you here so I..."

The old man rattled on and on but I wasn't listening anymore. You couldn't believe half of what the old man told you when he got into his euphoric, I'm-the-best-guy-who-ever-lived stage of drunk that usually showed up when he was drinking vodka but when he said I was going to live with Cindy, I believed him. He couldn't have found that part of his story in a bottle. For the first time in a long time, maybe for the first time in my life, I was excited about the way my life was going.

I was yanked back from the 1870s and the blue mountains of Colorado by the unmuffled sound of a motorcycle accelerating off in the distance. I looked over and saw a single headlight bobbing through the sweeping curve of the main drag into town about a half a mile or so away. Folding over the corner of the page I was on, I reluctantly put the book back in my suitcase and resigned myself to staying in the present.

The old man had said Cindy would meet me at the bus stop but the bus had been running about four hours late when we pulled into town. I hadn't been surprised to see she hadn't waited around and figured she'd probably just check back every hour or so until I showed up. I didn't think it was very likely that she'd be riding a motorbike but anything was possible. I hadn't seen or heard anything about Cindy in over five years.

The motorcycle driver downshifted as he passed the village limit sign and the bike rolled into the confines of the silent little town like an angry dog growling after a stranger. Another downshift and the bike's exhaust barked an occasional backfire that grew from loud to almost scary as it drew closer and the sound began to echo off the buildings around me. The driver finally noticed me sitting on the curb and accelerated slightly as he swerved to the right before pulling a u-turn to sweep around and stop directly in front of me. I stood up and took a couple steps back up on the sidewalk as the bike died in front of me with one last gunshot-sounding backfire.

The bike was a mildly chopped street machine with leather-fringed saddlebags, a two-tiered, low bar seat, and high rise handlebars. The driver was every father's nightmare.

Everybody has a set of stereotypical pictures of the tattooed and leathered guys who make up a motorcycle gang; the skinny, kind of ratty looking guy who's tough in a group but nothing on his own, the fat sloppy bald guy who's just plain mean and stronger than any other fat guy you ever see in real life, and the long haired, quiet, serious looking guy with slab muscle arms and washboard stomach who is obviously the meanest and toughest guy in the bunch.

The guy glaring over at me from the seat of his bike fell squarely in the middle of that last category.

"Well?" he asked in an impatient, raspy voice.

I studied the man's face looking for the question he wanted answered but all I could see was hair. The man wasn't wearing a shirt; he either spent a lot of time in the sun or he was part Mexican. The belt running through the loops of his well-worn jeans was a thick, heavy metal drive chain of some kind and the engineer boots on his feet were black, heavy and scuffed. A faded tattoo of a semi-naked woman reclined across his right, thigh-sized bicep, a smashed June bug was tangled in his chest hair and the sour odor of his sweat took precedence over the gassy, cooked oil smell rolling off the bike's immaculate engine. The motorcycle itself- a long, low slung, evil looking thing with tapered flowing lines and bulbous headlamp- looked like a bastardized crossbreed of machine and giant praying mantis. I couldn't find a single thing about the man that appeared even remotely friendly.

Looking around impatiently, he glared back over at me.

"What's your name, asshole?" he rasped sardonically.

"Ken," I answered.

"Well it's about f[illegible]g time, Ken," the guy

responded, running a hand back though his hair. "Get on."

I hesitated for a split second. The man hadn't even mentioned Cindy's name. I considered asking him a few questions but immediately thought better of it. If the guy were looking to make me his bitch he sure as hell wouldn't have wasted any time asking my name.

I collected my bags and stepped up to the bike as the man jumped up and slammed the kick-starter down. The engine burped into life and barked a couple times as my chauffeur revved the engine before letting it fall off to a rough, incredibly loud idle that I could actually feel reverberating inside my chest. Taking a deep breath, I tried to figure out how to get on without scratching the bike (an offense that I figured would probably rank right up there with killing this guy's mother) or touching the guy (something I just plain didn't want to do) but came up empty. I was just about to ask if I could put my suitcase inside one of the bike's saddlebags when the man glared over at me and revved his piece of American iron.

"GET ON!" he yelled, straining his raspy voice.

I spied a foot pedal just above the muffler, put my foot on it and swung my leg over the low back bar without scratching the bike or touching the guy. Unfortunately the guy clunked the bike into gear and hit the juice before my butt hit the seat and I ended up dropping my paper sack in a brief, frantic struggle to stay on the machine. Grabbing at the bottom of the bike seat with my left hand, I found a purchase and hung on for dear life as we roared out of town. Now, I'm not normally left handed but my right hand had a death grip on my suitcase full of books. I knew I could get by without the clothes I had been carrying in that paper bag but my books were important to me and I wasn't about to let them go.

The rest of the ride was uneventful but still terrifying. Scooting my butt back to the back bar, I managed to prop my suitcase up on the seat between the driver and me where it couldn't pop open and concentrated on staying on the bike as we flew along the road. Remembering the June bug splattered on the guy's chest, I quickly closed my eyes and kept them that way until we slowed and I felt the bike leave the blacktop.

Opening my eyes, I saw we were idling into the gravel parking lot of a small honky tonk bar surrounded by what looked like fields of corn. The bar was a rundown two-story building with three dilapidated cars nosed up to the wall and a very dated neon sign hanging from a pole out next to the highway. The sign alternated between flashing CHARLEY'S in yellow neon, to flashing a blue martini glass complete with green olive. The bent neon tubes that formed the letters H and E in CHARLEY'S were burned out, along with half the length of the red neon toothpick that was sticking out of the green olive, but you got the idea.

The guy pulled the bike up to the cracked sidewalk that led up to the front door of the bar and stopped.

"Get off," he rasped without killing the engine. I climbed off the bike carefully but quickly and waited for further instructions.

"Cindy's inside," he said, revving the bike. "Tell her I'll be back in an hour."

The guy shifted the bike and took off.

"Thanks for the ride," I called out sarcastically and very, very quietly. Like the old man said, I was a smart ass but I wasn't stupid.

I set my suitcase down on the ground and looked around as the roar of the bike gradually dropped off and disappeared under the sounds of the frogs and insects singing in the motionless fields around me. Someone inside the bar dropped a nickel in the jukebox and the muted base line from a slow country song vibrated softly through the walls and joined in with the music outside. Halfway through the song I picked up my bag, walked away from the front door and out into the parking lot.

After looking forward to this moment for five days, I was suddenly scared to see my sister and I didn't know why.

I worked the problem over in my head as I paced along behind the cars parked next to the building. I had been excited about seeing Cindy, still was as a matter of fact, but I had never stopped to consider the fact that I didn't know this girl anymore than I knew the man on the moon. We had been born seven years apart so we had never really been what you would call friends, Cindy had always been far more mature and sophisticated than I ever was, nearly level with mom and dad up on that lofty plateau of adulthood in my adolescent eyes, then she had dropped out of my life. I suddenly realized I had never known the girl who had left, let alone the girl who had been gone for five years, and now I was suppose to drop down in the middle of whatever life she had made for herself and expect her to take care of me. My own dad couldn't take care of me for crying out loud, how had I ever fooled myself into thinking that moving in with my long lost sister would ever work out any better? The turn in my life that I had been so excited about back in California now looked as though it didn't have a chance in hell of being anything but a giant dead end complete with a five hundred foot drop off on the other side of the guardrail at the end of the road. I was wandering around out in the parking lot because I didn't want to get any closer to the edge of the cliff than I already was.

A wedge of light and music suddenly spilled from the front door of the bar and a woman stepped outside. She was shorter than I remembered and her hair was different but I knew right away that it was Cindy.

"Kenny?" she called, peering blindly out into the night.

The door behind her snickered shut and a helpless wave of panic enveloped me. Time suddenly doubled up on itself and overlapped in a clean line. The five years separating the day Cindy had left and this exact moment just fell away and were gone. I was nine and I was fourteen. I was a kid but someday I would die.

My heart hammered in my chest as I stared at Cindy from the safety of shadows while her eyes adjusted to the night. The soft, alternating glow of yellow and then pink neon from the road sign washed over her face, its warm shades separated by a split second of dark. In the yellow light of the word CHARLEY'S I could still see the face of the girl I had grown up with, in the pink glow of the martini glass I saw a young version of our mother. I opened my mouth to answer but couldn't speak. I stepped out around the back of the car and walked toward my sister.

"Oh my God," Cindy said quietly, catching sight of me. We came together and I felt the weight of responsibility and loneliness slip from my shoulders as we hugged. For a few brief seconds I was a child for the last time in my life and Cindy was there to protect me as I cried silently in her arms.

"Hey, hey, hey," Cindy whispered. "I've missed you too, kid."

I guess Cindy and I held each other for less than a minute that night in the parking lot of a bar which no longer exists but it was a minute that meant a lot to me and one that I can still see and feel even now nearly thirty years later when I close my eyes to this waiting machine in front of me and think about it.

I finally took a deep ragged breath and stepped back to look at my sister.

It was obvious the previous five years hadn't been easy ones for her. Her face, while still pretty and unlined, looked hard and guarded somehow. A thick, inch long scar that had long since healed, curved over her left eyebrow, and her nose, which I remembered as being perfect, curved noticeably to the right. Her long red auburn hair had been cut short and straight.

"Hey, you're kind of short to be a big sister," I said, smiling down at her.

"Hey, you smell like you haven't had a shower in about a week," she smiled back. "How was your trip?"

"Better than a jab in the eye with a sharp stick," I answered, using one of the old man's favorite lines. "But not by much."

"God, I've missed you, kid," Cindy repeated, stepping back to look at me with sparkling eyes and an impish little half smile that used to belong to our mother. "Look at you! You're as tall as dad now, aren't you?"

"Taller," I smiled. "But I never bothered pointing it out to him."

"Well, I don't blame you there," Cindy nodded her head.

We both knew the old man did not like to lose... at anything. I learned this pretty early on in life when he taught me how to play checkers. The day I won my first game was the last day the two of us ever played. Pointing out that I was taller than the old man was would be like winning at some kind of competition and then rubbing his nose in it. There just wasn't any percentage in doing that.

"Look at your hair!" Cindy said, pulling my hair out from one side of my head and exposing one ear. "He must have noticed you were bigger than he was to let you get away with this."

"Not exactly," I smiled. "I had it stuffed up in a baseball cap every time he saw me."

"Get out of here," Cindy laughed. "You did not."

"Honest injun," I smiled, holding up two fingers. "I didn't see him that much so it wasn't hard and when I did see him he had other things on his mind."

"Speaking of Sheila, Cindy said, wrapping her arms around her waist and looking disgusted, "is that woman as ditzy as she sounds over the phone?"

"Yep," I nodded. "But you should see how she fills out a sweater."

"I figured it was something like that," she said. "You men are all pigs."

"Hey," I protested.

"All right, all men except for you," Cindy smiled. "You're just spooky."

I immediately had a mental flashback to six or seven years earlier. I was sitting cross-legged on my bed trying to make sense out of an analogy I had overheard the school librarian make to a teacher's aid (something about the similarity between chickens and kids, I think) when suddenly I felt someone staring at me. I turned around and saw Cindy leaning there against the door.

"What are you doing?" Cindy asked, looking perplexed. "You haven't moved in ten minutes."

"Thinking," I shrugged.

Cindy just studied me for a couple of seconds and then smiled.

"God, you're spooky," she said, only the way she said it made it sound almost like a compliment. I grinned back at Cindy and felt that warm good feeling only a younger sibling can feel at being accepted, even if only for a minute, by his idol.

I smiled at the memory as the two of us stood there in the parking lot looking at each other. Neither of us knew what to say next but it was all right. We were family and we were together, that was enough.

"That guy that picked me up said he would be back in an hour," I said, finally breaking the silence. "Who is he anyway, a friend of yours?"

"My husband," Cindy answered, her smile draining away. She held up her left hand to show off a tiny diamond ring. "Jim."

I waited for her to say more but that was it. No "Jim... the love of my life," or "Jim... he looks mean but he's really just a big teddy bear," or even "Jim," with a smile. I felt my stomach do a back flip as I pictured myself stepping over the guardrail and inching closer to the drop off. If Cindy wasn't getting along with her husband now, having me around sure wasn't going to help.

"So how's the old man?" Cindy asked, changing the subject. "You know, he actually sounded sober over the phone."

"Shit," I said, dragging the word out sarcastically. "He might have slowed down a little a few months ago but he was making up for it when I left."

"Oh, yeah?" Cindy gave me a worried look. "The way he talked I figured he must have quit altogether. How did he manage to buy the house?"

Warning lights started going off in my head and I could see little pebbles rolling and bouncing down the face of my metaphorical cliff. I pulled out my crumpled cigarette pack and fished out the last smoke.

"The old man told you he was buying a house?" I asked, my heart sinking in my chest. I knew the old man and I already had a pretty good idea what was coming. I pulled out my matches and lit up. "When did he tell you that?"

"A couple of weeks ago when I called to ask... to see how he was doing. He told me he would have to call me up next time because you guys were moving into a house and it would probably be awhile before he could get a phone hooked up." Cindy pulled out her own pack of cigarettes. Her hands were shaking. "He called me from a pay phone last week to tell me he was sending you up here for a week or so while he and Sheila got settled and..." Cindy turned around, took a couple of steps away from me and looked up at the sky with one arm wrapped around her waist.

It was pretty obvious the old man had pulled something over on Cindy but I had my own fish to fry. Had she just said the old man told her I was only staying for a week?! How could he do something like that? He told me I was going to live with Cindy and he told her I was just visiting for a week! What did he expect me to do, just weasel my way into overstaying my welcome by three or four years? I felt like someone had just kicked me in the stomach.

"He didn't send any money with you, did he Kenny."

There wasn't any question in Cindy's voice. She knew the old man as well as I did.

'GERONIMO!' an inner voice yelled as I mentally stepped off the edge. I walked over to the closest car in the parking lot, a rusty Chrysler Newport, and leaned back against the door.

"The phone was disconnected before I left because there wasn't any money to pay the bill," I answered, looking down at the gravel at my feet. "Sheila's car was repossessed last month and they're probably about two weeks away from being evicted. There isn't any money."

Cindy kept her back to me and didn't say a word. I didn't care. I couldn't feel anything. I wasn't scared, I wasn't mad at the old man; I didn't even feel sorry for Cindy. I was empty.

"Kenny?"

Cindy was standing in front of me, studying my face.

"Dad told me he'd loan me a thousand dollars and he was going to send it with you," she said, a single tear rolling down her cheek. "I thought it sounded too good to be true but I wanted to believe him, I wanted to believe that he had changed, I guess. I..."

"CINDY!" Light spilled out onto the grass and some drunk yelled from the doorway around the corner of the building. "PHONE'S RINGING IN HERE!"

Cindy walked over to the corner of the building.

"Go ahead an answer it, will you Red?" she said, her voice hitching a bit. "If it's for me tell them I'll be right in."

"YOU GOT IT SWEETHEA..." Red yelled back, closing the door on his own reply.

Cindy picked up my suitcase and walked back to me with it in her hand. "I'm sorry, Kenny," she said, holding it out to me. She suddenly looked as beaten as I felt. "You aren't going to be able to stay here."

Ignoring the suitcase, I struggled to understand what Cindy had just said. Had she really just told me I had to leave? Why couldn't I stay? I hadn't done anything to her; it was the old man that had screwed her over. I was just a kid, for crying out loud, where was I going to go?

"I can't stay with you?" I asked, stepping away from the car. "Not even for the night?"

Cindy looked directly into my eyes and shook her head.

"I'm sorry," she said. "But if you're here when Jim gets back he'll hurt you."

"Me?" I said. "I didn't do anything, why would he hurt me?"

"Because he's going to be in a lot of trouble when he can't pay some people the money he owes them tomorrow and he's not going to believe the old man didn't send that money with you. He's going to think you have it and he'll try to beat it out of you."

"But you believe me don't you?" I said. "Can't you tell him what a shit the old man is? We could tell him to search me... he could go through my suitcase. If I leave now it will just look like I did take the money, won't it?"

"Listen to me," Cindy said, shaking her head and grabbing my hands with her own. "I don't have time to explain things to you. All you have to do is hitchhike back down the highway here to Grand Rapids. Go to the bus terminal and show them your ticket back to California. Give them some song and dance about how there was no one here for you to stay with and I'm sure they'll work something out for you. Okay?" Cindy looked at me and pleaded with her eyes. "You can do that can't you?"

I didn't know what to say. I didn't have any money,

food, or cigarettes and my bus ticket had been a one-way pass, not a round trip ticket. I had a suitcase full of paperbacks and the clothes on my back. Hell no, I couldn't do that. I needed someone to take care of me, someone to care if I lived or died. I opened my mouth to say as much but stopped at the pain I saw in Cindy's eyes. I could see she didn't want to do this any more than I did. There was something going on here that she didn't want me to know and I figured the scar over her eyebrow and the way her nose was bent to the right had something to do with it.

I looked down at the hands holding mine and saw how much smaller they were than my own. This little girl had only been sixteen when she got pushed out into the world, less than a year and a half older than I was now. Life couldn't have been easy for her then and it was almost certainly not a cakewalk right now; she didn't need an albatross of guilt over me adding to the troubles she already had. I knew it was time for me to be a better man than my father had ever been to us... but knowing that didn't make leaving any easier.

"Sure," I said, forcing a smile. "I can do that."

Cindy smiled back but didn't look any happier.

"God, I'm sorry," she said, dropping my hands and giving me a hug. "We'll get together again someday, I promise. Okay?"

"You bet," I whispered, not trusting my voice.

We stepped apart and started walking slowly toward the highway.

"Oh, damn," Cindy said, grabbing my hand and stopping. "You must be starving to death. You've got to have something to eat."

"No, I'm alright," I said, my stomach feeling anything but hungry. "I think I might as well just get going."

"What about money?" she asked. "I've got some tips inside, let me..."

"That's okay, Cindy," I said. "I've got a couple bucks, don't worry about it."

"Are you sure?" she asked. "You don't need anything?"

"Well, I am out of smokes," I admitted, stopping on the shoulder of the road. "I'd bum a couple cigarettes if you can spare them."

Cindy pulled an open pack of Marlboros out of her apron pocket and handed them to me.

"There's a machine inside," she said. "I'll buy another pack."

"Thank you," I said, looking down at my sister. God, I didn't want to go. "Thanks a lot."

Cindy stood up on her tiptoes and kissed me on the cheek.

"I love you, little brother," she said and then she was gone. She walked to the bar, opened the door and disappeared inside without looking back.

"I love you too," I said, whispering the unfamiliar words to the closing door.

Taking a deep breath, I picked up my suitcase and started down the highway.

One of my mom's favorite sayings when I was growing up had been 'God works in mysterious ways'. Anytime something unexpected popped up, good or bad, mom would shake her head, make a little 'tisk' sound and say, "God works in mysterious ways." The old man, on the other hand, preferred the phrase 'son of a bitch' for the same occasions. To me the two phrases were pretty much interchangeable and I never gave much thought to either of them.

I hadn't walked more than a foot or two out of the halo of light from the flashing bar sign before I realized I couldn't see a damn thing.

"Son of a bitch," I muttered, stopping dead in my tracks.

'God works in mysterious ways,' Mom's voice countered in my head. Suddenly, for the first time in my life, I saw the literal meaning in mom's little catch all phrase and it really pissed me off.

"Oh yeah, right mom," I retorted sarcastically. "God's working overtime in mysterious ways for me tonight, isn't he? Look, he went and made it dark out here so I can't see! Yes sir, old God is doing a bang up job for me all right."

I stood where I was and waited for a few more words of wisdom from my mom but didn't get any. Dropping my suitcase, I swore quietly and, for about the thousandth time since she died, I tried to understand why I was so angry with my mother.

"I'm sorry," I mumbled to her memory. "It's been a lousy day."

Picking my suitcase back up, I took a cautious step forward with my right foot and heard it crunch on the gravel just off the edge of the blacktop. Taking another step, I felt my left foot come down on the smooth, even surface of the blacktop.

"There you go," I congratulated myself. "Keep one foot on the road and the other on the shoulder and you'll do alright."

I took a few more steps and found the process worked out pretty well. One foot or the other would occasionally land on the lip between the tar and gravel but it was easy to correct and, as long as I took it easy, I wouldn't have any trouble finding my way down the road.

I can't begin to tell you how much it hurts me now to remember my distant fourteen-year old self walking along that dark deserted country road in the middle of the night with nowhere to go. The forty-three year old man that I am now can't help but feel a need to somehow reach out to that kid lugging his old battered suitcase and give him a hug; tell him that things will eventually work out and explain to him that he's not the one to blame for being on his own. I'd like to do these things but I know in my heart that the kid I once was would never be able to understand. I couldn't see my predicament through the eyes of an adult back then and, as hard as it may be to believe, I wasn't feeling sorry for myself that night. I was scared, of course, and I was pretty pissed off at both of my folks for deserting me, but I never once felt any self-pity. Finding myself on my own at fourteen was just one of those unexpected, kick in the balls type of experiences every kid lives through as they grow up. While we all find out in one way or another that life isn't always fair, some of us just learn earlier than others that it can sometimes bite you on the ass really, really hard. For the quiet, introverted kid that I once was, this particular bite just appeared to be a little bigger and a little deeper than the other scars on my butt. I guess I was just too young to know any better.

Walking the line between blacktop and gravel was slow going but I wasn't too worried about making good time; I didn't really have anywhere to go. I just trudged along the road with my head down and tried not to think of anything other than the next step down the road. Unfortunately the overactive imagination I had been born with wouldn't cooperate. The same three subjects kept popping up over and over in my head until they were finally condensed down to a marching cadence that my brain recited in time with my footsteps:

Mom is dead
Dad's a drunk
Cindy can't help me

Over and over again this morbid little jingle played in my head for every eight steps I took. I found I could get rid of it for a few minutes at a time by concentrating on thinking of other things (wondering what kind of animals were responsible for the foreign sounds I was hearing out in the dark topped the list) but the second my mind started to wander the jingle would sneak right back in and start all over again like an annoying little song. I prayed for a car to come along and stop for my thumb, a car with a talkative driver, a loud radio, or barking dog; anything to distract me from that nauseating rhythm but the road remained desolate and black. I finally decided the only thing to do was to stop walking.

Stepping off the road a couple of feet, I propped my suitcase up on one end and keeping most of my weight on my feet, cautiously lowered my butt down onto it. Pulling a cigarette from my breast pocket, I struck a match and lit up. I was shaking the match out when I heard a quiet 'chirp' somewhere above my head and glanced up. I couldn't see anything in the dark, of course, but for the first time in my life I could see what the night sky actually looked like without the light of a large city surrounding me, and it took my breath away.

I felt like I was looking up at an ocean. An ocean of black that held countless little particles of light suspended and floating everywhere I looked. There were millions, maybe billions of stars scattered above me, more than I could ever hope to count. An individual star, brighter than its neighbors, would quickly grab my attention only to slowly fade amongst the appearance of first hundreds, then thousands of other pinpricks of light surrounding the brighter star that would have otherwise gone unnoticed. The number of stars began to increase exponentially as motionless swirls of dusty white light scattered randomly across the sky hesitantly revealed their source of myriad individual stars along with the hint of more in the softer shade of black behind them. A shiver of panic ran down my spine as a sense of weight and substance grew in the vast canvas above me and I suddenly realized that I was nothing more than a miniscule germ walking on the surface of a planet dwarfed by the infinite space it was floating in. I was alone and my life was insignificant. I had to look away.

Finishing my smoke, I tossed the butt into the ditch, picked up my suitcase, and started back off down the road. An hour or so later the moon peaked over the horizon behind me, casting a pale whisper of light over the road but I was too tired to move any faster.

Like mom said: 'God works in mysterious ways.'

The first car traveling in the direction of Grand Rapids blew past me and my thumb just before daylight. The next three passed in quick succession about an hour later. I knew I was in trouble.

If I had to guess I'd say the temperature hadn't dropped below seventy or so during the night; an hour after the sun came up it had to have been eighty-five in the shade. The curvy, tree-lined lane I had been walking along the night before was now a radiant strip of hot asphalt bisecting identical fields of dry, stunted corn, and the thought of my last drink of water, a short pull off a public fountain back in a Des Moines truck stop some thirty-odd hours earlier, haunted me with its brevity.

As I watched the fourth car speed away (a cream colored Volkswagen Bug that had slowed just enough to trick me into breaking into a trot before accelerating away), tiny bubbles of exploding light suddenly swarmed across my rapidly shrinking field of vision as a gut-wrenching wave of nausea rolled over my body. Dropping my suitcase, I lowered myself to the ground, knelt on the shoulder of the highway and leaned forward to rest my forehead in the weeds. My stomach hitched once but I managed to fight it back down and immediately felt better for it. Taking long, deep breaths, I kept my head on the ground for a few more minutes before cautiously setting back and opening my eyes. The road, along with its bookends of cornstalks, swam in front of me for a second or two before settling down again and snapping into focus and, other than a minor headache, I discovered I felt okay again. Relieved, I slowly changed positions to sit back on my butt, lit a cigarette and considered what I should do next.

It was obvious that I wasn't going to be able to go much farther without some water to drink but where was I going to get some? I had passed three houses that I knew of during the night (there may have been others- the three I saw were the only ones that had left a light or two burning) but I hadn't seen anything other than corn since daylight. I looked down the road in front of me for a bridge or any other sign of water but couldn't see anything promising at first. Shading my eyes with my hand, I squinted against the sun and made out what looked like a stand of trees a mile or so away. The thought of getting out of the sun and relaxing in the shade seemed like a much smarter plan than staying where I was and baking my brains. Taking one last drag off my smoke, I stood up and, after squashing the smoldering butt with my foot, started for the trees.

As it turned out, the 'mile or so' I figured I had to walk to get to that stand of trees was a lot closer to five miles than one and by the time I got close enough to distinguish the individual leaves on the trees, I was feeling pretty lousy. My minor headache had developed into a hammer on anvil type of pounding, my body felt strangely hot and clammy at the same time, and every minute or so my vision would vibrate and scramble as if someone were adjusting the rabbit ears on a TV. On the plus side, I could see a mailbox up ahead of me on the right at the far end of the tunnel of shade. I decided to forgo the relaxing under the trees for a chance at getting some water from the house that had to accompany the mailbox and pushed on through the shade without stopping. Stepping back out into the sun five minutes later, I let my bag drop to the ground and looked at the house I had been betting on.

The damn place looked abandoned.

The house, or at least what I could see of it through the branches of two towering pine trees, was a very old looking, two story farmhouse set about a hundred feet or so back from the road. The paint was peeling and mostly gone, a small outbuilding between the tree line and the house looked like it had collapsed years earlier, and the weeds that made up the yard were about up to my knees. A large weathered barn standing behind and to the left of the house looked more than a little spooky with rusty brown hulks of abandoned farm implements slowly sinking into the weeds and bushes that surrounded it. I looked over to the mailbox to check for a name and saw that any sign of what might have once been written there had apparently rusted away years earlier. The only thing I could see that gave me even a glimmer of hope was an old black Ford pickup parked at the top of the gravel driveway. The old Ford looked almost as abandoned as the house beside it and could have easily been sitting there for months or even years without moving but I could see that all four tires were still inflated. I glanced over to the driveway on my left and noticed several sets of tire tracks left from someone driving in and out since the last rain.

I was just bending down to pick up my suitcase when I heard a woody sounding 'whack' across the weedy yard from somewhere near the house. Two seconds later I saw the figure of a man walk around from the back corner of the old building and head toward the truck. I snatched up my bag and hurried down the driveway to intercept him.

I hadn't quite made it halfway to the truck when the man noticed me coming. He stopped where he was next to the driver's door of the decrepit looking vehicle and gave me a good looking over while waiting for me to reach him. I was close enough by now to see that the man was old and kind of ornery looking. Not wanting to take a chance on pissing the man off by making him wait for me any longer than necessary, I flashed what I hoped was a winning smile, gave a little wave and broke into a labored trot. My stomach immediately did a slow roll and my legs suddenly felt decidedly rubbery but I ignored them both.

"Excuse me," I puffed as I slowed to a walk a few feet away from the back of the old man's truck. "I..." and that's all the farther I got. My vision tunneled down to a pinprick in a heartbeat, my legs turned into noodles and I felt myself start to fall. That was it. Everything just went away.

It was raining. I could feel the drops splashing off my skin and hear them smacking into the ground around me. I didn't know where I was but that wasn't important; my head hurt too much to try and figure it out. The only thing that mattered to me at that moment was the rain. Tilting my head back a little, I opened my mouth to catch the falling drops and quench my terrible thirst. The thought of opening my eyes floated by but I decided to keep them closed against the chance I was dreaming.

"Can you hear me, boy? Come on, son, wake up!"

I opened my eyes a little against the falling rain and saw the vague silhouette of a person standing at my feet. I squinted down for a better look and saw an old man. Satisfied I had found the source of the quiet voice I had just heard, I closed my eyes again.

"Well shit," the man sighed quietly.

I kept my eyes closed but heard something drop to the ground and the rain stopped an instant later. Opening my eyes a slit, I saw the man was walking away. I looked back down at my feet where the man had been standing and saw a spray nozzle screwed onto the end of a garden hose. It hadn't been raining at all- the man had been spraying water on me to cool me off! I looked back over at the old man and saw a familiar looking rundown farmhouse beyond him. Everything came flooding back.

"Sir?" I called weakly to the man. "Sir?"

The old guy stopped and looked back at me. I gave a weak wave and watched as he turned around and started back. Still not feeling on top of the world, I laid my head back down on the wet grass and closed my eyes. The man seemed to be standing over me in the same instant.

"I was just going in to call for the meat wagon," he said, his quiet voice barely audible. "How you doing?" I opened my eyes and looked up at him.

The old man stood just this side of being small, if he stood over five foot four I would have been surprised, but the sinewy, muscular arms hanging from out of his short sleeved shirt went a long way in adding to his stature. His clothes alone (brown polyester dress slacks and a faded, button up print shirt) were proof enough that he wasn't a young man anymore but other than that, he hid his age well. The lines in his tanned, weather beaten skin looked more like cracks and creases in a well worn piece of leather than wrinkles brought on by age and his hair, while mostly hidden beneath a dented tweed hat, was just showing the first signs of gray. The man could have been an old looking forty-five or a remarkably young looking eighty; it was impossible to tell.

"I'm not sure," I answered. "Not too good, I guess."

The old man stared down at me for a long second before giving me a little nod and walking over to my feet. Bending over without the usual groan I had always associated with old folks, the man picked up the sprayer, stood back up and turned it on me. My mouth dropped open on its own and I couldn't help but gulp at the drops I could catch.

"Sun stroke," the man stated, raising his voice just enough for me to hear over the spray. "And you're going to want to stop that."

"Stop what?" I gasped.

The man narrowed the spray down and concentrated it on my chest and waist.

"Swallowing that water," he answered. "It'll repeat on you."

I was having a hard time following what the old man was telling me but I suddenly realized I was too sick to care. With a feeble attempt to roll onto my side, I puked up what little water I had been able to swallow.

"There you go," he said in a told-you-so kind of way. I didn't say anything; the realization of just how sick I really was had just started to sink in and I was getting scared.

"Roll over, boy."

I groaned and tried to do as the old man had said but only managed to scare myself even more with the realization that I didn't have the strength. What the hell was wrong with me? I opened my mouth to ask the man to bring me to a hospital but the world winked out again before I had the chance.

"And the actual price of your showcase is... Four thousand one hundred AND TWENTY ONE DOLLARS SARAH JANE ASHMAN YOU ARE OUR SHOWCASE WINNER OF THE DAY!!!!"

I stared mindlessly at the image of an overweight black woman, apparently one Sarah Jane Ashman, doing her level best to squeeze Bob Barker to death while lifting him off his feet. The television audience roared and clapped as canned music rose up in the background. Bob Barker, wearing a slightly strained smile on his face, valiantly struggled to extricate himself from the overly enthusiastic winner and turned to face his camera.

"From all of us here at CBS, this is Bob Barker saying goodbye and asking you all to please join us again tomorrow on... The Price is Right!! Goodbye everybody!"

Bob waved and the credits rolled. I blinked my eyes and for the second time that day, wondered where the hell I was. Without moving my pounding head, I could see I was lying on a floral patterned couch and according to the mantle clock sitting on top of the console television across from me, it was straight up four o'clock but that knowledge didn't help me any. Short, wispy clips of events were flirting on the edge of my consciousness but looking at them straight on was like trying to pick up a drop of mercury from a broken thermometer; they just squirted away. I lifted my head and looked around.

"Still alive, eh?"

I jerked my head around toward the familiar sound of that quiet voice and saw an old man sitting in an overstuffed easy chair next to the couch I was lying on. He didn't have his tweed hat on but I immediately recognized him as the guy with the hose and a few of those wispy memories suddenly snapped into focus. I scrambled around on the couch in spite of my headache, lifted the sheet I found covering me, and looked underneath. I didn't have any clothes on! What the hell?!

"Oh, take it easy, boy," the old man sighed, getting up out of his chair. "There aren't any ladies about."

I watched the man carefully as he walked across the floor in front of me, around the corner of the L-shaped room we were in and on in to the next room. Keeping the sheet wrapped tightly around me, I sat up and leaned over to see what he was doing.

The next room turned out to be the kitchen. I watched the man as he opened a cupboard door, took down a glass and walked over to fill it at the kitchen sink. The old guy stared absently out the window over the sink as he filled the glass; he didn't look down until the water overflowed and started running over his hand. Turning off the spigot, he dumped a little of the water out and carried it back into the living room.

"See if you can keep this down," he said, handing me the glass. Walking back over to his chair, he sat down and stared at the television where another game show, Matchgame '74, was just getting started. I went ahead and drank my water, but I kept an eye on the guy while I did it.

"There's a phone," the man said. He glanced over at me and nodded to a space between his chair and the couch I was on. I leaned over the arm of the couch and looked. The phone was there all right, sitting on a short table next to an overflowing ashtray. I sat back on the couch and looked at the TV.

"Ought to give your folks a call, don't you think?"

the old man asked a couple minutes later. I stared at the TV and considered how to answer him. The guy had probably saved my life that morning so I supposed I probably owed him at least a halfway truthful answer, but at the same time, the idea of telling the old man, the same old man who had stripped me naked while I was passed out, that I could drop off the face of the earth and no one would ever even notice... well, that just sounded like a very bad idea to me. While the sum total of my knowledge about what perverted old men liked to do with boys like me was pretty shaky at best, I was pretty damn sure it had something to do with getting the kid's clothes off.

As I struggled with my dilemma my right hand instinctively went to where my breast pocket should have been and patted my bare skin for my pack of smokes. I remembered the water spray soaking through my clothes that morning and realized my nearly full pack of smokes had probably gotten soaked. I looked over at the old man and found him watching me. He looked back at me silently for a couple seconds before reaching into his shirt pocket and pulling out a pack of unfiltered Chesterfield shorts, 'lung rapers' my dad used to call them, and a Zippo.

"How old are you, boy?" the man asked quietly. Shaking out a cigarette, he plucked it from the pack with his lips before offering the pack to me.

"Sixteen," I lied, taking the pack from his hand. The old man's steel gray eyes focused on me for a second before clicking the Zippo open and thumbing it into life.

"Bullshit," he said, talking around the dangling cigarette in his mouth. He put a little more emphasis on that particular word than any of the others he had spoken so far but it still came out just a decibel or two above a whisper.

I shrugged my shoulders and pulled a cigarette from the pack. The old man handed me his lighter and I lit up. Taking a deep drag, I blew a perfect smoke ring toward the ceiling before snapping the Zippo closed and handing it back to the man.

"What's your name, son?" he asked, seemingly unimpressed with my ring of smoke. I took another drag off my cigarette as I stared at the TV.

"Richard," I exhaled, glancing over at the man. "Richard Riley."

The man considered my answer for a second before looking back to the TV. We both stared at the screen as a goofy looking male contestant began to pick which three of the six stars on the Matchgame panel he wanted to ask for help in filling in the blank.

"How about...Nipsey Russell...Charles Nelson Riley... and, of course, Richard Dawson." The goofy guy clapped with the studio audience and nodded confidently.

I kept my eyes glued to the screen in front of me but I could feel the old man turn and stare. I felt my cheeks getting warm and knew I was turning red. I was busted. The old man squashed his cigarette out in the ashtray, got up out of his chair and walked over to the television set.

"All right, Richard Riley," the man sighed. He snapped the set off and turned to face me.

"I'm going to drive out to the cemetery now and visit my wife. After that, I think I'll swing by Charley's for my supper and a beer. I'll probably be gone an hour or so. If you want to leave while I'm gone, go ahead. If you can find something worth your while to steal on the way out," the old man turned and gestured to the room around him, "have at 'er - everything I've ever cared about is already gone." The old man paused and looked down at the floor. A second later, his eyes snapped back up and he bored ahead.

"You can shit or go blind for all I care, Mr. Riley, but if you are still here when I get back, you'd better be ready to tell me your real name and maybe a little something about how you ended up lying half dead in my driveway. You lie to me again, I'll be helping you out the door with a good swift kick in the ass, you hear?"

I stared up at the man, dumfounded. How could anyone give an ass chewing like the one he had just given me without ever raising his voice? I couldn't understand how he did it but there was no doubt in my mind that he had meant every word he said.

The man looked at me hard for a second longer before shaking his head and turning around to leave. By the time he reached the doorway to the kitchen, I knew what I had to do.

"Why'd you take my clothes off?" I called.

The old man stopped and stood where he was for a second before turning around to face me.

"Washed 'em," he said. "They were muddy and, if you remember, you puked on your shirt."

I considered the man's answer for a second and decided I believed him.

"I'm fourteen," I said. "And my name is Ken Malone."

The old guy looked at me silently for another long second.

"Martin Ash," he nodded grudgingly. "Pleased to meet you."

The old man turned and started for the door. I heard the 'whack' of a wooden screen door slamming and, a minute later, the sound of his truck start up and reverse down the driveway.

From my perch on the couch I looked around the room as the sound of the old man's truck faded away outside. The house grew silent except for the evenly spaced ticking from the clock sitting on the television set and the occasional bird chirp from outside the windows. It was an odd sensation, being in a stranger's house by myself. I wrapped myself up a little tighter in my sheet and tried to decide what I should do. The phantom pain of being homesick for a home that didn't even exist any longer hit and I remembered the phone sitting on the table next to me.

The desperate thought of calling my dad or maybe my sister was suddenly all encompassing; I actually started to reach for the phone before catching myself. I pulled my hand back and quickly banished the idea from my head before it could grow into a need that could only end up hurting me. Dad didn't have a phone and he apparently didn't want to hear from me anyway. Cindy probably wouldn't mind if I called down to Charley's to tell her where I was, but what good would that do? It looked like she had more than enough troubles on her own with motorcycle Jim there and, as far as she knew, I was riding my return ticket home back to the old man. Calling Cindy might have made me feel better but it would only worry her and it wouldn't help either of us.

I finally settled on picking up the receiver and holding it up to my ear to listen for a dial tone. The phone worked all right but knowing that didn't make me feel much better; my head hurt, I was scared, and I was alone. The magnitude of being entirely responsible for myself suddenly towered in front of me and I realized it was up to me to figure out how to climb it. A picture of my mom walking through the doorway of our apartment in Detroit popped into my head and I was helpless to stop it. I watched as she slipped her key back into her apron pocket and she smiled over at me sitting in front of the TV. I knew the pillowy aroma of beer, grease and cigarette smoke would reach me a second or two before she did when she walked over to kiss me on the head. I longed for even a minute of the past, a minute of sitting with her again, listening to her tell me about her day and asking me about mine.

"NO!" I yelled, driving the memory away. Moping over mom right then wasn't going to accomplish anything and I knew it. Getting a fresh grip on my sheet, I stood up, picked up my water glass and walked out to the kitchen.

Filling my glass at the sink, I drank my water looking out the same window over the sink Mr. Ash had been looking through earlier. The yard outside the window looked like hell. There wasn't a blade of grass in sight, only weeds, dried out and apparently dead, swaying silently in the breeze.

The idea of asking the old man if he'd hire me to mow his yard popped into my head and I quickly decided it was a good one. The man seemed to be a decent enough guy and I thought it pretty likely that he'd let me spend a night or possibly even two on his couch. I might not have ever pushed a lawn mower before in my life but I had watched other guys do it before; how hard could it be? Refilling my glass, I decided to approach him with the idea when I got a chance and then quickly shelved the idea away to keep from getting my hopes up. I stared blankly out the window and drank my water.

It seemed odd to me to look out a kitchen window and not see a bare brownstone wall five or six feet away. An apartment with any kind of view in the city warranted an extra five or ten dollars a month in rent and Leo Malone wasn't one to pay extra for anything he couldn't drink. I kind of enjoyed the feeling of being able to see so far and wondered what it felt like to have all that empty space outside your door just waiting for you every day. There were parks in the city, of course, but they belonged to whoever decided to use them and a lot of those people were pretty strange. I never spent much time there.

Finishing my water, I set the glass on the counter next to the sink and looked around. I still had a headache but it was a lot better than it had been a few minutes earlier and I was suddenly famished. I walked over to the fridge, a surprisingly new model compared to everything else I had seen in the house, and opened it up, looking for something edible that Mr. Ash wouldn't miss. With the exception of a row of condiments on one of the door shelves and a single can of beer on the middle shelf, the fridge was bare. No wonder the old man went out to eat. Looking a little closer at the condiments, I found a jar of pickle slices and pulled it out. Being a little neurotic about how long things could hide in a refrigerator, I checked the date written on the cap, did a double take, and shuddered. August 21, 1969... the damn pickles hadn't been edible for five years!

I carefully replaced the jar and eased the door closed.

Working my way down the cupboards, I opened them one at a time looking for any dry goods that might be there but came up empty. The only sign I found that there might have once been food in the house was a single empty cupboard, the rest held pots and pans and dishes. Giving up on finding anything to eat, I decided to look around for my clothes.

The kitchen I was standing in was the heart of the old farmhouse. The room wasn't that big, maybe ten foot by twelve, (it looked even smaller with the kitchen table sitting in there instead of out in the wide open dining room ten foot away) but I still counted four doors in addition to the wide entryway that opened to the L-shaped dining room/living room that held my couch. I could see from where I was standing that the open door across from the sink led to a small mudroom and the back door. The other three doors were closed.

I started with the door on my left and found Mr. Ash's bedroom. I took a quick peak around to make sure the washer and dryer weren't tucked away in one of the corners and closed the door faster than a Pavlovian dog answering a bell (by the time I was seven, my snooping around in places where I had no business being had turned up three of the old man's hidden vodka bottles and I, or more specifically, my butt, had paid dearly for each one. I had learned my lesson well).

The next door I tried opened to reveal a steep set of stairs leading to the second story. The smell of mothballs, dust, and time did its best to entice me up the stairs to take a look but I fought the desire back and closed the door. The next door led to the largest bathroom I had ever seen. The room looked as though it might have been a bedroom back when the old house had a 'path out back' for plumbing but it had evidently been converted over some years ago. An old and not very clean washer and dryer set sat partially hidden on the other side of the metal shower stall directly in front of me. I opened the dryer and found my clothes. After closing the bathroom door, I dropped my sheet to start getting dressed but stopped as I remembered what Cindy had said the night before about my not smelling very good. The thought of a long cool shower was heaven. I walked over to the stall and turned on the water.

Stepping out of the shower, I dried off with a towel I found folded under the sink and got dressed. I had done some thinking while the water cascaded over my body and it had occurred to me that Mr. Ash could use a kid like me for more than just yard work. If he was anything like my old man, he didn't have a clue about how to cook; I had started cooking the odd meal for mom and myself after moving to Detroit and had pretty much cooked everything I ate after moving back in with my dad. And Mr. Ash's house, while neat and orderly, appeared to have not seen a dust rag or had a window washed in years... probably since his wife died, I guessed. I knew how to dust and clean and, as long as I was getting paid to do it, I could do a bang up job.

The old man was living alone and as far as I could see, he wasn't a very happy camper. Even if the old guy turned out to be an ornery cuss, that single can of beer I had seen in the fridge told me he wasn't a drunk (while my old man preferred liquor- "Liquor is quicker," he'd say occasionally when he was in his cups, he wasn't above buying a six pack every now and again and none of those six beers ever saw a shelf life of more than an hour). I figured staying with him for a while would be a cakewalk compared to what I was used to.

I walked out of the bathroom feeling great; my headache was gone, five days of dirt and sweat were washed away, and I had a plan. The only thing missing was a cigarette. On the off chance Mr. Ash had noticed my smokes and saved them before spraying me down, I looked around for my suitcase and found it in the mudroom. Setting the suitcase flat on the floor I opened it. No cigarettes. I sat there for a minute looking at the jumble of books lying inside and got an inspiration. I grabbed the L'Amour paperback I had been reading earlier, opened it to the first page (an advertisement for other Louis L'Amour books) and tore out the sheet of paper. After fishing out a book of matches I set the suitcase back against the mudroom wall where it had been, walked back into the living room and grabbed the ashtray full of butts.

Back when I was about nine or ten I developed an unquenchable need to smoke (I can't explain it so I won't even try). I would have bought a pack of cigarettes if I had any money (a five-year-old with enough smarts to tell the clerk he was buying them for his old man could have bought cigarettes back in the sixties) but since money was scarce and I was still a year or two away from having the balls to snitch a butt or two from the old man's pack, the only thing I could find to smoke was coffee. Every free minute I had without adult supervision was spent learning how to roll cigarettes using notebook paper and coffee snitched from mom's three-pound Hills Brothers tin. By the time I graduated to real cigarettes, I was pretty good at rolling my own.

I already knew there weren't any keepers in the old man's ashtray before I picked it up, checking for butts worth smoking was second nature to me and I had automatically checked the first time I looked at it, but seeing as how Martin smoked filterless cigarettes, each squashed butt had a good pinch or two of unsmoked tobacco. Picking out five or six of the largest butts, I walked back through the house and out the backdoor.

I stepped out on the small wooden back porch outside and looked around at Martin's backyard as the screen door whacked once and settled in its frame. It was still hot outside but a breeze had kicked up since morning and the porch was nearly completely shaded by the house. I walked across to the portion of porch rail still out in the sun and leaned up against it. I just stood there for a while and watched the birds, bugs, and bees zipping around above the weeds. It felt strange to be able to look out across the back yard to the field and woods beyond and see so much and so far without seeing any people. I stood there for a minute trying to take it all in but the sight kind of gave me the willies. I let my mind go for a second and let myself imagine I was the last surviving person on the planet but had to rein the thought in almost immediately... the quiver I felt run down my spine at the imaginary scene hit a little too close to home. Looking away, I walked over to the porch steps, sat down and started collecting tobacco.

I finally managed a presentable cigarette after going back inside to tear out another page (the title page this time) from Louis' novel. The size of the cylinder might have been closer to a cigar than a cigarette but it was fairly uniform and, as a surprise bonus, I had inadvertently managed to end up with the title of the book, *Passin' Through*, printed down the length of my hand-rolled smoke. I smiled a little when I noticed it, but without someone to show it to, it wasn't all that cool.

I pulled out my book of matches, struck one and lit up. Settling back against the well-worn stairs, I smoked my cigarette and tried not to think too far ahead.

According to my mom, I was born a month premature for the simple reason that I just decided I wanted out. I don't recall anything about it, of course, but I tend to think she was probably right. I spent the better part of my childhood feeling like a small but powerful portion of my brain was an entity onto itself- a kind of self-contained big brother in my head, one that never slept and always seemed to know more than I had a right to know. The idea that this big brother entity had grown impatient to get the more feeble systems it was hardwired to out of the womb and online sounds perfectly plausible to me.

I was a quiet baby; I seldom cried and when I did it was never for more than a minute or two. I took an immediate and obvious dislike to certain individuals on sight and, again, according to my mom, I was usually an excellent judge of character. I started talking when I was six months old but only in front of my mom or Cindy and only when they were alone. I usually refused to smile when prodded to do so and always refused to do so on the few occasions I had my picture taken. Mom used to have nine Polaroid snapshots of me as a baby and believe me, I was one ornery looking little bugger.

My memories from the numberless four years that passed before I started kindergarten have long since deteriorated down to either things that I just know to be true- memories without specific images or instances to back them up- or, in a few rare cases, short little vignettes of pictures and sound without benefit of setup or ending. Remembering one of the latter is something like switching on a TV and watching five or ten seconds of whatever show happens to be playing before turning it off again. You might come away with a sense of what the program was about but most of the time you wouldn't.

One of the things I can remember without really knowing how I know is this; mom always seemed to be a lot happier when the old man wasn't around. And, while I'm pretty sure I loved my parents equally back then, I know I felt better when he wasn't around too. I never had to worry about whether mom liked me or not.

One of the apartments we lived in before I started going to school was a small, one bedroom walkup. The living room/dining room and kitchen were all one room with an old couch marking the border between them. Mom and dad slept in the only bedroom, Cindy had a small bed set up for her in the living room, and I slept in the bathtub. I know what that sounds like- sleeping in a bathtub- but it really wasn't bad. Every night my mom would take two of the three cushions off the couch and put them in the tub before covering them with half of a bed sheet. As soon as she finished I'd shimmy over the edge, drop down inside my porcelain cocoon, pull the other half of the sheet over myself and wait for mom to seal the deal by shaking my blanket out high above the tub and guiding the comforting weight of the thing to float down over me. I remember I liked sleeping there but I doubt we lived there for more than a couple of months so it didn't last.

I did a lot of my TV watching in this apartment while sitting on the floor with my back against Cindy's bed. One day (almost certainly after the old man left for work) I discovered a new way to amuse myself. Every time a commercial interrupted Kookla, Fran, and Ollie, Romper Room, or whatever show it was I happened to be watching, I'd get up, tear around the perimeter of the room (we didn't have squat for furniture; the only two things I had to avoid were an ashtray stand and the ratty looking, tub-cushion-supplying couch), somersault on and over Cindy's bed and land on my butt in the exact spot on the floor where I had been sitting seconds earlier. I'd then repeat the process for every commercial that ran until the program came back on. I don't have any idea how many circuits I ran around the living room during the two or three months we lived there; every second of every trip was melded together, homogenized, stored away in a little compartment up in the still uncluttered attic of my brain and labeled, Fun Thing I did as a Kid, back when I was about ten. All of the stocking footed trips I once ran, every innocent yet childishly arrogant lap run to the commercial jingles of Winston cigarettes, Chevrolet Malibu's, and Maxwell House Coffee, are now embodied in one hazy representative memory... except for one.

The program I was watching faded to black. A commercial! I scrambled up from the floor on my self-imposed cue and took off running.

My sock covered feet skidded sideways on the hardwood floor as I rounded the first corner but I didn't care; the floor was inches away, falling hardly ever hurt. Coming out of the corner unscathed, I sped down the long straightaway past the room dividing couch with my big boy legs pumping and the still new sound of wind rushing past my ears. I heard a noise behind me, started to look back, but it was too late; I had reached the far end of the room. I slowed slightly and started into the turn with a minimum of foot slippage. The noise was still there. Unwilling to stop, I shot a wide-eyed, open mouth glance behind me and saw my mom. She was laughing, running awkwardly, her eyes sparkling and alive as she struggled to keep her footing. Mom was chasing me! I laughed a high-pitched peal of delighted fright and rounded the curve into the home stretch. Mom was gaining, drawing even. The bed loomed closer and closer. I jumped. She jumped. We flew through the air, tucked our heads and somersaulted on and over Cindy's bed to land on the floor in unison with a satisfying 'WHUMP!' that rattled the windows in their frames. I looked over at mom in shocked wonder. Her hair was mussed, her cheeks flushed. She was laughing and her eyes sparkled and danced. My mom looked happier than I had ever seen her look in all the time I had been her son.

"I always wanted to try that," she grinned.

And that's it. That's all I can remember. I have other little memory snippets of my mom stored away but this one is different from all the rest. This was the one and only time I ever had a chance to see my mom for the person she might have been, the carefree, vibrant girl she could have been, had she married someone other than my dad. This was the one time I ever saw my mother truly happy... and it only lasted about ten seconds.

God, that still kills me.

By the time I started school a year or so later, I (or, to be more precise, the seemingly all knowing and omnipresent entity that governed all that I said or did as a child) had decided that no one would ever have the kind of power over me that the old man seemed to have over mom... except I never thought about it that way. I wouldn't make the connection between my parents' unhealthy relationship and my burning need to question authority until after their divorce. I just knew, as every other creature on this planet somehow knows, I had to follow my instincts if I wanted to survive.

I taught myself how to read before I started going to school by studying my mom's weekly copy of The Grit but I never told anyone. The Grit was a simple, Reader's Digest version of a newspaper if there ever was one. Armed with alphabetical information gleaned from Captain Kangaroo, I sounded out words and committed them to memory while pretending to use my crayolas to fill in the coloring pictures printed in the kid's section of the paper. I had asked my mom to teach me how to read once but she turned me down and told me I had to wait until I started school. I never asked my dad if he'd help me; something just told me that asking him would be a mistake. I wouldn't find out the old man didn't know how to read until Cindy told me years later.

I was in kindergarten when I walked up to the teacher's desk one day during naptime to ask permission to go to the restroom. The teacher (Miss Booth, a bony woman with bad teeth and a reedy voice) told me no and I was instantly one pissed off little five- year-old. It wasn't so much the fact that she turned me down (I really didn't even have to go, if you want to know the truth- I just hated the whole concept of a forced naptime), it was the way she turned me down that ruffled my feathers. She didn't offer any explanation or allow me the benefit of a moment or two of thoughtful consideration. She never even looked me over to see if I was holding my crotch or jumping from one foot to the other the way some of the dumber kids in the class did when they really had to go. She just said no and that was it and I couldn't see a reason in the world why.

"Well, I'm going," I said, and I turned on my heel and walked out.

Right or wrong, Miss Booth never said or did anything about it.

A librarian busted me once when I was in the first grade for stealing a book from the third grade reading section of the elementary school library. I had asked this same librarian's permission to check out a book from the older kids' section the day before but she had turned me down cold; I didn't see that I had any other choice. I was tired of Dick and Jane and their stupid dog. I wanted to read books with substance, books like the few Cindy brought home from time to time when she said she had to do something called a 'book report'. I wanted to read books that contained more words on one page than the sum total of every word (including copyrights and publishing company logos) of all four of the Dick and Jane works combined. I had read my fill of nouns and verbs and the seemingly inexplicable word 'the'; I craved adjectives, adverbs, and prepositions, I hungered for the odd dangling participle. I didn't know what any of those things were yet but I desperately wanted to learn.

The next day I waited until the person I now thought of as my enemy was distracted by another kid, walked up to a third grade level rack of books, and slipped one of them down the back of my pants. I would have gotten away clean except one of the other kids in the library saw me do it and squealed. The librarian checked me over, found the book and personally escorted me down to the principal's office where she left me. Five minutes later, after a flawless reading of a page the principal had picked from the book at random, I walked back down to the library with an authorization slip from the principal to check out any book I wanted. I was in heaven but the librarian was plenty steamed. She did all she could to pick on me after that (if you're still young enough to remember what the combination smell of puke and that purplish crap they covered it with was like, you can probably still recall knowing the cold fact that some teachers were actually the worst bully in the class) but my family ended up moving across town to a different district a little while later so it didn't really matter.

In every grade at every school I attended, I inevitably ran into a senseless rule or an adult who felt he or she deserved unquestioning respect and I questioned every one of them. Sometimes I lost. Most of the time I won.

Outside of my quest to rebel against any and all incompetent displays of authority, I was just another kid. I was precocious but I hid it well. I never volunteered an answer in class, I never asked any questions, and I never sassed anyone. My only downfall was I always scored straight A's.

The sixth grade marked the beginning of the California School System's initial foray into separating the smarter students from the slower ones. Being in the smart classes really cut into the amount of time I could read in class. The classes themselves weren't that much harder for me than any of the other classes I had taken (I never had to study or listen to the teacher more than five or ten minutes to understand what was being taught on either level), it was the teachers that changed. The class sizes were smaller than the regular classes which allowed the teachers to keep a hawk eye on everyone; reading anything other than the subject being taught was not allowed. This was unacceptable to me. Why should anyone care what I did as long as I was scoring straight A's? I tried talking to the teacher about it but I might as well have been talking to my Lost in Space lunchbox. I thought it over on my walk home from school that night and came up with a plan. By the end of the first marking period that year my grades had taken a nose dive and were hovering right down there in the meaty part of the curve; straight C's. My mom caught it right away and bugged the hell out of me for a couple weeks asking me what had happened. If the old man noticed he never said anything. We all moved to Venice Beach before the end of the next marking period and I was delighted to find I was not placed in any of the advanced classes in my new school and neither of my parents ever had to sign the back of another report card that carried a letter grade higher than a C.

True to his word, I heard the old man's truck chugging up the driveway to the house a couple minutes after six. I got off the couch where I was watching the news ("Impeachment proceedings scheduled for President Nixon" the anchorman had just announced breathlessly; I couldn't have cared less) and walked out to the kitchen where I leaned against the sink to wait for him.

"Still here, eh?" Mart said. He stopped inside the mudroom to wipe his feet on the rug as the screen door slammed behind him. I immediately noticed the grease stained, white paper sack the old man was carrying and my mouth started to water.

"Here you go," he said, handing me the bag.

Stomach growling, I took the bag, peaked inside and saw a huge cheeseburger wrapped in wax paper sitting on top of a bed of french fries. While the hamburger smelled like heaven, I cringed a little at the sight of the fries beneath it; I had eaten far more than my share of french fries back in Detroit. The man who owned the bar where Mom worked made her pay for any food she ate or brought up to me except for french fries. French fries were peeled and sliced up daily down in the bar's kitchen and any fries that hadn't been cooked up for customers by closing time were going to get thrown out anyway so the owner of the bar didn't begrudge mom the three or four hundred orders she brought up to me over the year we lived there. I hadn't had a single fry since mom had died (to this day, the smell alone makes me feel both poor and slightly nauseous) but I was too hungry to be picky.

"Sit down," Mart said. He pulled a chair out from the table and nodded to the one opposite for me. Impatient to get started I pulled the chair out, sat down and went after my food. I ate everything except the paper bag it came in.

"Guess I should have ordered two," Mart said stone-faced as I finished.

Still chewing, I swallowed my last fry and looked across the table at the man. I'd been so busy eating I had forgotten he was there. I hadn't even thanked him. Reaching into his breast pocket Martin pulled something out and tossed it across the table to me- a pack of Marlboro reds along with a book of matches slid to a stop next to my elbow. The matches had the word 'Charley's' printed diagonally across the front flap.

"I would have taken your smokes out of your pocket before turning the hose on you if I'd noticed them, but I didn't." Mart pulled a Chesterfield out for himself and spun the wheel of his Zippo. "Figured you'd prefer your own brand," he said, gesturing at the pack of Marlboros with the flaming Zippo.

"Thank you," I said, tearing the cellophane ripcord from the pack. "For these and the food." Mart just nodded and flicked the ash from his cigarette.

The two of us sat there at the kitchen table and smoked. A breeze picked up outside and whistled through the limbs and needles of the twin pine trees out in the yard. The sound of a car rumbling past out on the blacktop rose up and dropped off as quickly as it had appeared. A fly buzzed and bounced at the window screen searching for a way out. The clock in the living room ticked slow seconds away and a drop of water lost its tenuous grip and fell from the kitchen spigot to the porcelain sink below.

I guess everybody who lived back in those seemingly ultra-modern days of the seventies has a memory or two that defines that decade for them. The five or six silent minutes Mart and I sat at that table in 1974 is mine. The Vietnam War had been all but lost, Nixon was two weeks away from resigning the presidency, and the price of gas had shot up to over forty cents a gallon. The whole country seemed to be a little shaky and uncertain but it was still a relatively quiet place and we all knew there was a bigger, better world just around the corner. We had put a man on the moon over five years ago, for God's sake! The whole world had watched live telecasts of men walking and driving cars around up there! Anything was possible now...it was just a question of when. Technology was revving up around every corner, you could feel it chomping at the bit, straining to break free to begin knocking down the barriers of isolation and ignorance that insulated small communities and individual homes from the hectic, noisy pace of expansion and progress. Computers, cell phones, wars played out in real time on television; they were all just science fiction back then but they were coming...you could feel it. Colors were brighter, surfaces were smoother, and, even if you couldn't afford it, somebody had gone out and invented an oven that cooked your food in seconds using something called microwaves. There was even some talk of having twenty or even thirty TV channels wired directly into your home over a cable rather than picking them out of the air with an antenna. It wouldn't be free, of course, but what the hell; what were a few bucks compared to boredom? Never again would we have to sit in silence, listening to the sound of life and time tick quietly by. Technology would take all that away for us at the press of a button, who could ever settle for anything less?

"Call your folks while I was gone?" Mart asked.

Having been lured into a kind of hypnotic state by the peaceful quiet, I jerked a little at the sound of the man's voice.

"Ah...no, I didn't," I answered, sitting up in my chair. Mart waited for me to go on but I kept my mouth shut.

Lying to the old man was about the last thing I wanted to do after the ass chewing he had given me earlier that day, but telling him the truth wasn't without some serious risks. If I told Mart everything and he decided to take it upon himself to call someone to report me as a runaway or abandoned kid or something, my ass would be in a foster home before I knew what hit me and I couldn't let that happen. Besides that- but on another, more subconscious and murky level somewhere between instinct and a conscious decision- I felt a strong need to protect my old man from looking like he didn't care what happened to me. Questioning or even thinking about this jagged little sliver of need was out of the question; digging it out would have meant poking into places that were far too bruised and tender to be disturbed. I just knew that if Mart got too nosy about what he needed to know, I was going to have to leave.

"Don't suppose you're on the run from the law, are you?"

Surprised at the question, I looked up at Mart and saw he was smiling. His smile wasn't a big toothy grin or anything like that, it was actually closer to a smirk, if you want to know the truth, but it was a smile just the same and I was glad to see it.

"No," I answered, smiling a little myself.

Mart nodded. Leaning forward, he squashed his cigarette out in the ashtray.

"I guess I should tell you I took a peek inside your suitcase while you were out there on the couch," he said, sitting back in his chair. "I was hoping to find something with a phone number or address on it so I could call your folks and have them come get you."

Mart paused and waited for a comment but I wasn't biting. The clock out in the living room ticked away. Another car rumbled past out on the road. Unlike ninety-nine percent of the adults I had dealt with in my life, this old man wasn't afraid to let a minute or two go by without having to say something. Silence had always been my ace in the hole when it came to dealing with anyone I perceived as having some type of unearned authority over me but I could see my weapon of choice was impotent against Mart. The old man was as comfortable in silence as a cat napping in the sun; he reveled in it. I couldn't help but respect him for that.

The old man pushed himself up from his chair and walked over to the refrigerator. Opening the door, he bent down and snagged the single can of beer inside.

"Sorry I don't have anything to offer you," he said, walking back to the table. "Mary and I used to know damn near every single person that lived in this county and most every one of them stopped in here looking for a beer or a cup of coffee at one time or another. Mary was never one to let a person leave this house wanting."

Mart set his beer down on the table and eased himself down onto his chair. Scooting the chair forward, he propped his elbows on the scarred tabletop and reached for his beer.

"Course they're all dead now," he said, popping the tab and dropping it into the ashtray. "They're all gone." Mart raised his beer and took a drink from the can before setting it back down and pulling out another cigarette. "And if it weren't for you and that suitcase full of books," he said, giving me a narrow look as he flicked open his Zippo, "I'd have gone to my grave and joined them a much happier man." The old man thumbed the wheel, held the flaming lighter to his cigarette and lit up.

I studied Mart's face looking for the punch line. The old man squinted against a wisp of smoke as he tucked away his Zippo and met my gaze with one watery blue eye. The man was dead serious.

"I guess I don't understand," I said. "What did I do?"

Mart looked down at his cigarette and tapped the ash with his little finger.

"You and your books reminded me of a time in my

life when a friend of mine needed help but I was too young to do any helping," he answered slowly without looking up.

"I'm sorry," I said, not knowing what else to say. The old man didn't seem to be making a whole lot of sense. "I just wanted a glass of water." Mart looked up at me and I saw another hint of a smile.

"Not your fault," he said, shaking his head. "Like my ma always told me; 'God works in mysterious ways".

"Hey, my mom used to say the same thing."

As soon as the words were out of my mouth I saw my mistake. 'My mom used to say the same thing'...I might as well have come right out and told the old man that my mom was dead as to say something like that. It wasn't that I really minded if Mart knew my mom was dead, in fact, the old man never skipped a beat and seemed to have missed my gaffe completely, but the fact that I had told the old man something about myself without meaning too...well, that bothered me quite a bit. How could I ever hope to steer clear of do-gooders and their foster homes running off at the mouth like that?

"It's a line that covers a lot of ground," the old man nodded agreeably. "But personally, I've always been of the opinion that God has more of an odd sense of humor about him than a mysterious way. I guess the fact that he held back on my IOU for damn near 70 years before calling me on it shouldn't really surprise me."

I thought about it for a second and decided I didn't agree with Mart and his assessment of God. I'd done more than my share of thinking about God and his ways since my mom had been murdered for the hundred and seventy-two dollars that her killer had walked away with and I felt pretty confident that God, if he actually existed at all, did not have any kind of sense of humor that I could see.

"What was your IOU for?" I asked.

Glancing over at me, Mart shifted in his chair and noticed his cigarette had gone out. Tossing it into the ashtray, he pulled out another, tucked it into the favored corner of his mouth and lit up.

"I promised God I'd never turn my back on any kid who he saw fit to send my way and I asked the same from God in return," he answered, settling back and crossing his legs "You're the first kid to show up."

I studied Mart skeptically. I knew what religious nuts were like; I had two of them for grandparents. I hadn't noticed any resemblance between those two holy rollers and this chain-smoking old man before but now I had to wonder. Hopefully the old man was just kidding around; I carried a real big chip on my shoulder when it came to religious people. In all my admittedly limited experience I had found that religious people would claim they wanted to help you but their promise always came with some kind of price attached.

"Oh, come on," I eyed the old man suspiciously. "You're making that up."

"No, it's a fact," he said mildly. "And, judging from the library stamps on the side of most the books I saw in your suitcase, I'd say God went to a lot of trouble to get you here just to see if I'd hold up my end of the bargain. Let me tell you, son, you are hell and gone away from California and I'm guessing it's been one hell of a ride that brought you here. You better than anybody ought to know how you ended up keeling over out there my driveway this morning and, while I'm normally not much of a betting man, I'd be willing to bet the farm here that you didn't have much of a say in how you ended up in this neck of the woods."

I wasn't convinced. All this crap about Mart promising God that he'd help a kid if one showed up, it had to be a lie the old man had dreamed up to get me to tell him the gory details of my life. It was either that or the man really was a religious nut who hadn't quite gotten around to the telling me what the catch was going to be in exchange for his help. Either way, I wasn't going to fall for it. Okay, so maybe the sequence of events that brought me to this house were akin to flipping a coin and having it land on its skinny edge... about ten times in a row. Those long odds only counted if I were gullible enough to believe Mart had actually made this supposed promise. The old man had to be lying or, if he wasn't, my showing up at his house was just sheer coincidence. The God I conceptualized was a far cry from this picture of the interactive, caring kind of God Mart was trying to sell. A caring God would never have taken my mom from me. A caring God would have made sure I had a home. The God I was familiar with didn't give a rat's ass what happened to me; the very idea that he had taken enough of an interest in me or this old man to guide me to his house some three thousand miles away from where I started was laughable and I was tempted to let Mart know it. I settled on staring back at the old man and kept my opinions to myself; I figured I probably owed him at least that much.

"I don't know," Mart shrugged. "Maybe I'm wrong. Maybe you ran away from home because your folks told you to get your hair cut or maybe you got grounded for sassing your mom or hitting your little brother and you just decided to leave. Maybe you could pick up that phone right there and have somebody out here to pick you up five minutes after you ring off...but I doubt it. You play your cards too close to the vest, son... too close to be new at this business of watching after yourself.

"My life ended when my wife died three years ago. Every friend and neighbor I ever had is dead and buried and waiting for me up to the Sand Lake Cemetery and I'd like nothing more than to join them, but I'm still here. Everyone's gone and everything has changed and I've been ready to die since I dropped that shovel of dirt on Mary's coffin...but I'm still here. I must have asked God to take me home a thousand times over these last few years but he turned me down cold every time. I could never understand why until I opened your suitcase this afternoon and saw those books and that's when it hit me. I remembered David, I remembered the day his sister told me he was gone, and I remembered my promise."

Mart paused and put his smoke out in the ashtray.

"You are the reason I'm still here, son," he said, setting back. "I've been waiting for you to show up for over three years now without knowing it and now you're here. I've got a debt to pay before I can go to meet my maker and I'd appreciate it you'd let me balance the books. All you have to do is let me help you."

The old man had finally named his price. Oh, he hadn't come right out and said it in so many words, but it was there and I recognized it for what it was. I looked away and busied myself under the guise of lighting up a cigarette. I was pissed off and getting angrier by the second.

The old man didn't give a shit about me. He was offering to help me in the hopes that it would boost his position on God's hit parade. He was practically telling me I had no choice but to accept his help. Well, I had some news for the old coot; I didn't need anybody's help. All I had wanted out of the old man was a fair trade; a day or two of yard work in exchange for some money that I could use toward a bus ticket back to California...and that was still all I wanted, but Mart had gone and screwed everything up by telling me about this stupid promise he had supposedly made to God. Accepting anything from the old man now would be as good as an admission that I needed not only his help, but his God's help as well and I wasn't about to do that. Mart's God didn't exist or, if he did, he could kiss my ass. He had had plenty of chances to help me out before now and he hadn't done shit; I wasn't about to take the chance that I might be accepting any of his help now. Nobody was going to put a ring through my nose.

I decided it was time to hit the road. I collected my cigarettes and matches off the table and put them in my shirt pocket.

"I sure appreciate everything you did for me today," I said, standing up and sliding my chair back under the table, "but I guess I'd better get going."

I stepped around the table and held out my hand. The old man sat there for a couple seconds studying me before slowly pushing himself up from his chair.

"You're welcome, son," he said, shaking my hand. The old man's expression never changed but his eyes suddenly looked confused and old. I could see he knew he had said something to make me want to leave and I felt bad for him; all he had wanted to do was help. There was a brief struggle as the weak and vulnerable side of my soul tried to convince its ever-vigilant and protective counterpart that I should sit back down at the table and tell the old man everything. There was a time when that emotional, caring side would have won out too, but that time had ended the night before when I walked away from Cindy. Caring about how other people felt could only hurt me.

I turned from the old man and walked across the floor to the mudroom and my suitcase. Picking it up, I turned and looked back at Mart for what I knew would be the last time. The old man had turned to watch me go and started to take a step toward me. I took a step back and he stopped.

"You probably saved my life this morning," I said. "I don't know if you really made that promise to God or not, but if you did, I'd say you've kept your end of the bargain."

Mart opened his mouth to say something but I turned and stepped out the door before he could get it out.

I didn't notice the ominous clouds above me until after I had walked far enough and fast enough to take the edge off whatever self-righteous anger had driven me out of Mart's house. I might not have even noticed then except for the drop of rain that had just landed on my hand.

"Aw, son of a bitch," I moaned, looking up at the threatening sky. I dropped my head and turned around to walk backwards and look for any cars that might be coming up behind me but the road was empty and quiet. I had seen seven cars since I stepped out onto the blacktop and of those, five were going in the opposite direction. The two that were going my way had been polite enough to give me a wide berth as they passed but that was it. I knew if somebody didn't come along and pick me up in the next five or ten minutes I was going to be shit out of luck. Nobody ever stops to pick up an already wet hitchhiker in the rain. I paused long enough to tuck my cigarettes away in my suitcase to keep them dry and took off again.

I was exhausted. My legs were loose and rubbery, my suitcase was growing heavier by the minute, and even though I hated to admit it and would never have allowed myself to go back, I was having second thoughts about my reasons for leaving Mart's house. In fact, the more I thought about it the more apparent it became that I didn't even know what those reasons were. I thought I had left because the old man was a religious nut of some kind but that didn't hold water, the old man smoked, drank beer and I was fairly confident I had heard him drop a cuss word or two during our conversation. Sure, he had mentioned God, but he didn't even do that right. Martin talked about God like he was talking about a Governor he had voted for; he might like and respect the man but that didn't mean he couldn't tell a joke or two at his expense. When my mom's dad, the only real religious nut I had ever been subjected to, talked about God, he sounded like an S.S. Officer singing the praises of Hitler; walk in mindless obedience to the Fuhrer or die.

Unable to find support for what I thought of as my primary reason for leaving the old man, I began to consider the other, lesser reasons that drove me out the door. I remembered feeling like he was telling me I had to accept his and, by extension, his God's help, but that didn't fly either. While the old man may have already made the seemingly obvious assumption that I would accept his help before he offered it, the only thing he had really done was ask to help me. The very fact that he had offered to help me at all was more than enough to get my hair up and make me suspicious. Couple that with Mart's mention of God, the ultimate authority trigger for my ever-building resentment, in the same sentence and there you have it. A lost kid jousting with windmills...and the windmills didn't even exist.

I wouldn't realize for another couple years yet that my indignant reasons for leaving that day were all just excuses my brain manufactured in an attempt to build a wall between the old man and myself. Given my recent track record, who could have blamed me? Everyone I had ever loved in my brief life had turned me away or left me and allowing myself to trust a complete stranger to go out of his way to help me would have meant opening myself up for more of the same. Any competent, first year psych student could have diagnosed and explained it to me in about five minutes but I never would have listened.

The scattered raindrops had grown to a light shower

by the time I heard the next car coming up behind me. I pushed my hair back behind my ears, hoping to give the driver an impression of a clean-cut young man looking for nothing more than a ride to a Boy Scout meeting, turned around and stuck out my thumb.

The car was a mid-sixties, four-door piece of shit-probably a Pontiac Bonneville but it was hard to tell. Two of the four headlights were missing, the windshield was nearly opaque with cracks emanating from a good size starburst on the lower passenger side, and the back end had been jacked up in some misguided effort to make the once respectable family sedan look fast and mean. The muffler (if it had one) was shot; a dragging tailpipe was producing a solid wake of short-lived gold flashes that bounced and rolled across the road behind the car. The vehicle was a rolling deathtrap that no one with an ounce of self-respect would ever even consider driving and I knew if any driver was going to stop for me that night it would have to be this one. I took a step out onto the oncoming car's lane and waited.

The car was still about a quarter of a mile away when the driver let off the gas and the car began to slow. I tried looking through the windshield as the car approached but couldn't see a thing through the spidery maze of cracks. There was a fingernail-on-blackboard squeal of metal on metal as the driver hit the brakes and a piss-shiver of dread pinballed up my spine. I was suddenly struck by an overpowering urge to run. I stepped back onto the shoulder and took a quick look around. The stretch of road I was on had a cornfield on one side and a field of some kind of grass on the other, both too short to offer up any cover, and the nearest tree looked to be about a mile away. The ditches on both sides of the road were overgrown and dense but only about four foot wide; far too narrow to do any good now. I looked up and down the wet asphalt for another car but, other than the rolling deathtrap and me and my suitcase, the road was empty.

I turned back to the coasting Bonneville and saw two guys watching me through the front and back passenger doors. They weren't full grown men but they weren't kids either. Considering the condition of the car, it was a lead pipe cinch that the driver and anyone else who might be in the car were all about the same age- old enough to start trouble but too young to know where to draw the line. Get two or three of these boy/men together outside the restraining eyes of parents, teachers or anybody else who might give a damn and things could get out of hand in a heartbeat. A semi-innocent exercise of newfound power and intimidation between these guys and a lone, younger kid like me could turn into a beating... or worse. I edged a little closer to the ditch and watched the approaching rust bucket with the nervous eye of prey watching predator.

The old Bonneville's tired engine suddenly cut out and a dark but muffled Black Sabbath tune took its place, adding a surreal note of dread to the metallic brake squeal of the slowing vehicle. The driver hit the lights and one of the two headlamps still hanging in the battered grill flickered into dim life, illuminating the drizzle-wet asphalt sliding beneath the car with a soft weak glow. The guy in the back seat raised a mini bottle of Miller beer and chugged it down in about five seconds, tipping it up to drain the last few drops of foam as the wheels of the car rolled to a stop a foot or two short of where I was standing. I could see the driver, a kid about the same age as the other two, glaring at me through the shattered windshield as he pushed the column shifter up into park. Leaning over a little toward the passenger side, he raised his arm to the dashboard and Ozzie was cut off mid-howl. The world went suddenly silent except for the rounded tunking sound of raindrops splattering hollowly off the roof and decks of the Bonneville. The driver said something to the two passengers without taking his eyes off of me. The two exchanged glances and smirks but the driver's expression never changed. Putting his shoulder against the door, he worked the handle and shoved. The car rocked gently from side to side as the door clunked open and swung out with a protesting squeal. The driver climbed out of the car as the two guys left inside rolled down their windows. I bent my knees and set my suitcase down on the ground behind me as I studied on the driver.

Growing up as the perennial new guy, I knew my way around your standard schoolyard confrontation pretty well. I wasn't very big and I sure didn't look any tougher than your average sized, skinny white kid, but I had a brain and I used it. I learned early on that rule number one was always Never Back Down. Running to a teacher (or just plain running) would earn you numerous other fights with a whole slew of second string wannabe tough guys who would never have dreamed of screwing with you if you had stood up to the number one tough guy in the first place. Rule number one was followed by several other rules (Always protect your balls. Always throw the first punch. Keep hitting the other kid until he either gives up or some adult separates you, etc, etc...) but number one was, in my experience, the most important. I didn't win every schoolyard tussle that came my way but I never had anyone try to take me on more than once. Unfortunately, all of my fighting and confrontational experience had taken place in a school or in a neighborhood where there was always someone older and more respected to break things up. For about the hundredth time that day, I realized I was on my own.

The driver stepped around the front of the car and started toward me. His dirty blond hair was fairly short, not quite long enough to cover his ears, and cut in the shape of a soup bowl. He had a lantern jaw and a long, slanky mouth that looked too big for the rest of his face. While he didn't really look all that tough physically, he sure walked the part: tall, loose and easy. He was enjoying himself. He walked up to within a foot of me and stopped. One corner of his mouth was turned up in a friendly smile while his dark eyes remained cold and dilated. His nose looked like it had been broken more than once and his breath smelled like beer.

I knew I was in trouble.

"What are you doing out here kid?" he asked conversationally.

One of the guys back in the car snickered under his breath. The driver heard it and his smile widened. He glanced over to the car and bobbed his head a couple of times before turning back to face me. I heard another voice, a higher, quieter one this time and only for a word or two, but it was just background noise. My entire being was focused on the alpha male in front of me; I already had a good idea how this was going to end and every adrenaline-fueled cell was poised on the brink of flight or fight.

"Walking."

I didn't want to answer at all but I wasn't overly anxious to give the driver an excuse to start wailing on me either. We all knew I was going to come out on the loosing end of this deal sooner or later; the only option still open to me was to decide whether or not I was going to hit this guy before he got around to hitting me.

"Ah?" Bowl hair drew the word out as he cocked his head and eyed me suspiciously. He raised his right hand and shook his index finger at me. "I think you were hitchhiking." The sarcastic smile drained away and the guy's face fell lax as he sidled up closer to me.

"You were hitchhiking, weren't you."

There wasn't any question in the guy's voice. Back in the car, the same nervously excited guy who laughed earlier, laughed again. Bowl Head didn't turn to acknowledge his audience this time; my next answer would decide how quickly things were going to progress between us. He didn't necessarily want to get it on yet- this was foreplay for him, he'd rather dance around and toy with me awhile, showing off for the two mouth breathers back in the car while probing for weakness' which could be used to humiliate me before finishing me off with a beating. However, being the aggressor meant he had his own set of rules that had to be followed and rule number one was Don't Take Any Shit From Anyone Smaller Than You Are. My first answer had been a tad cocky for his taste; if he didn't get what he was looking for this time, he would forego the brass ring of total domination and settle on doing what he could to get his rocks off by beating me more severely than he would have had I cowered and squirted a couple tears. Backing down from this mental midget, even temporarily, was abhorrent to me but it was the only chance I had to get the upper hand. I broke off my trademark Kiss My Ass glare and diverted my eyes.

"Yes, sir," I said. "I guess I was."

I glanced meekly up at Bowl Head as his rubber lips stretched back out into a confident sneer.

"So you lied to me then, didn't you?"

I avoided eye contact and nodded my head submissively. Bowl Head shove-punched me in the chest and drove me back a step. More chortles floated over from the car as my antagonist took a step forward to stay within proper menacing distance of his quarry. I clenched my jaw and waited.

"What's that? Speak up, boy, I can't hear you!"

"He's sassing you, Jack!" laughing boy yelled.

"He said, '████ You!' Jack! I heard him all the way over here!" shouted the other mouth breather.

While it might have taken a second for the depreciating comment to sink in, Bowl Head (a.k.a.-Jack) was apparently a man with some deep-seated self-esteem issues and obviously didn't appreciate the insolent catcall of disrespect from one of his underlings back in the car. I saw his spine arch as his mouth tightened down to a thin bloodless line and I knew I was temporarily forgotten as the ramifications of the impudent remark sank in. Unfortunately for Bowl Head, I knew from experience that my second rule, Always Protect Your Balls, is one that most of your 'Pick on People Weaker Than Me' types never seem to follow and he was no different; he left his wide open.

"You wanna come over here and..." he growled as he turned his head toward the car. Ready or not, this was my chance.

Taking a short, preparatory step back, I reached out and grabbed his arms at the elbows as I pistoned my bony, right knee up into his crotch.

"AH-OHHh-!" Bowl Head's grunt of pain was quickly strangulated down to a dry heave as he dropped like a sack of potatoes and porpoised over onto his side. I followed him down, driving my knees into his back. Grabbing a hand full of greasy blond hair with one hand, I jerked his face up off the black wet asphalt and went to work on it with the other. My first punch squashed his already crooked nose. Blood fairly squirted down over his mouth, and his eyes, two wide-open exclamations of shocked comprehension, were teary and scared and never saw the next blow coming- a punch that landed high on his cheek and broke a bone or two rather than squashing some cartilage.

"HEY!" One of the mouth breathers yelled from the car.

"GET OFF ME!!" Bowl Head shrieked, struggling over into a fetal position.

"JACK!!" A girl (girl?) screamed.

The squeaks and clunks of car doors opening accompanied the hollow 'clop' sounds of my fist bouncing off Bowl Head's ears and, after he covered them with his open hands, the back of his skull. It only took three or four punches to the rock hard plate of his skull for me to realize I wasn't inflicting any real damage. I let go of the shank of greasy hair I was holding and reached around the man's neck to drag bloody fingernail furrows down each side of his face. The response was immediate and gratifying.

"AAAAAIEEE..." Bowl Head screamed and bucked underneath me. I grabbed another handful of hair with my left hand and started to reach back down for his face with my right when I caught a glimpse of movement on my left. I jerked my head up in time to see one of the mouth breathers take a flying leap right toward me. I didn't have a chance.

WHAM!

The impact from the mouth breather knocked me off Bowl Head's back and slammed me headfirst onto the unforgiving asphalt. I was scrambling to get back up even before my face had a chance to scrape to a stop but something was wrong; the world was suddenly sideways. I pushed my upper body up off the pavement with both of my arms only to have the hard surface of the road rise up on my right and smack me in the head. I was lying on the road. I could feel misty rain landing on my left cheek while wet bumpy blacktop supported the right. My eyes refused to focus and my body, along with the rest of the world, was hiccuping in a slow quarter rotation turn, over and over and over. I knew I wanted to get up but couldn't remember why. There were people around, I could hear them moving around and talking. They sounded...excited? Worried? Had I been in an accident? I didn't know and didn't care. I closed my eyes.

A noise. Loud. Rhythmic. A car engine.

"NO! We've got to take him to the hospital!" A girl's voice. Close. She was scared...crying, maybe.

"What do you want me to do about it, Amanda? Carry him on my back? Come on, we've got to go or Jack's going to leave us out here!" A guy's voice this time. He was scared too.

"Let him! What if he dies, Tony? We can't leave him out here!" The girl sounded scared to death.

"Alright, alright, alright," Tony answered. "Tell you what; its almost eleven so Jack's going to have to get you back to Maxon's anyway. As soon as you get there you can call the cops if you want, just try not to let Cheryl hear you, okay? All you have to do is call and say you seen this kid lying on the side of the road. Don't tell them who you are, for God's sake, just say what you've got to say and hang up. Okay? Can we go now?"

The car's engine screamed and backfired as someone...as Bowl Head (Jack- his name was Jack) revved it unmercifully over the red line. I had been fighting...fighting with Jack, but someone else had...had...

"But I don't even know where we are! Why can't we..."

"Stanton Road. Tell them the kid is on Stanton Road, about five miles east of Pierson. Okay? Jack's gonna kill me as it is! Let's go!"

The girl was really crying now. She sounded miserable. I opened my eyes a slit but the couple was too far off to my right for me to see anything other than two shadowy shapes out of the corner of my eye.

"Alright," the girl sniffed. "God, why didn't I just stay with Cheryl?"

"Don't worry." The two shapes were moving away. "The kid just got knocked out. People get knocked out all..."

The voice was lost under the sound of the idling engine. A car door opened and slammed shut and the engine changed notes as Bowl Head dropped it into gear. I waited for the car to roll past me as it accelerated away but something was wrong; the car accelerated away all right, but it didn't pass me; it drove away from me. Bowl Head and I had been fighting in front of his car, how could he have taken off away from me like that without backing up a couple times to turn around? I guessed he might have swung the car around while I was out of it on the pavement, but I didn't think so. I might have been wrong, but it didn't seem like I had ever really lost consciousness...not completely...I didn't think...

I opened my eyes. What the hell had I just been thinking about? It seemed important but...but maybe it wasn't. I had been in a fight, I knew that much. I had been in a fight only someone else had hit me...someone had jumped me and my head had hit something hard and the people I had been fighting with left me here but it was okay because some girl (Anna? Mandy?) was going to call someone (Amanda!)...Amanda was going to call... the police!

I had to move. I rolled over and pushed myself up onto my hands and knees. The entire planet beneath me slowly rolled to the right, snapped back, rolled again, and then snapped back and caught. Worried about the nauseous feeling that was snaking its way through my guts, I cautiously raised my head and looked around without moving anything except my eyes. After finding the earth had finally settled on one specific plane, I pushed myself to my feet and started looking around for my suitcase. I don't know how long it took for me to find it (that metronome portion of my brain that had constantly monitored the passage of time for me in the past seemed to have jumped a cog or two) but, when I did finally stumble (literally) across it, I found it was on the wrong side of the road from where I expected it to be. I looked around for anything familiar that might remind me which direction I wanted to walk but it was hopeless. I couldn't see a damn thing. I had an inkling that I was facing the direction I had been traveling so I took off.

"Son of a bitch!"

A branch from a ditch tree jabbed my cheek as I walked off the road and onto the shoulder. Wiping the scratch with my palm, I stepped back a couple paces, straddled the edge of the blacktop and shoulder and, for the second time in as many nights, tried again.

Mom's voice was silent that night but she was there...I know she was.

I walked.

My body was running on autopilot, my brain on standby. I had a knot on the side of my head that appeared, at least to my gently probing fingers, to look like the better part of a cue ball... a cue ball with a pulpy, blood caked crater in the top center. There wasn't a whole lot of pain but the entire right side of my face felt oddly tight and, for awhile anyway, the night took on the texture of one of those cheap, often repaired and usually worn out films that schoolteachers used to run back in the days before v.c.r.'s. Sounds were distorted, time would jump ahead to splice two widely separated minutes, and the night would periodically slip out of focus before snapping back a few seconds later.

Sometime that night- without considering why- I walked off the road and stood in the ditch at the sound of a slow moving car coming up behind me. I watched through a patchwork of branches as the narrow cone of a spotlight flared into life and jerked hesitantly across the road from one side to the other. I didn't crouch or make any attempt to hide; I just stood there in the brush holding my suitcase and watched as a long, slow moving Michigan State Police cruiser idled by. The car windows were down and I could hear the voice of one of the two cops inside talking ("...damn phone is right next to the bed for God's sake! Tell me the truth: Could you sleep next to a ringing phone for...") over the slick sucking sound of the powerful car's wide, glass belted radials rolling along on the damp blacktop.

I walked. I didn't think, I didn't plan, I didn't wonder. I walked without seeing, aimlessly crisscrossing the road from one shoulder to the other before righting myself. My state of fugue gradually lifted but I wasn't interested in taking advantage of it; life was so much easier with my brain quiet. I was exhausted, hungry and sore, and traveling to a strange city through country that was foreign to every other place that I had ever known... but none of that mattered as long as I kept on walking. The mindless, endless and repetitive steps ahead of me were my salvation. There was the occasional animal noise but the noises didn't concern me. I noticed the lights of a house up ahead on my left but didn't care; I didn't slow, I didn't worry about anyone seeing me, I didn't even stop to wonder if they might have a dog. I trudged along without a sideways glance. I had to keep walking.

It was the sight of the mailbox in front of the house that stopped me and forced me to think. The rusty gray box was standing sentinel well outside the fuzzy crescent of light spilling from the windows beyond. I glanced at it without thinking as I approached, looked again, longer this time, and slowed to a stop.

The mailbox looked identical to the one out in front of Mart's house...but no, that couldn't be right. I had walked away from Mart's house hours ago and I sure as hell hadn't been walking around in circles. Okay; I might have been knocked a little silly back there when those guys stopped to give me a hard time but...

I looked up the overgrown yard beyond the mailbox and recognized Mart's house. My head rocked as the internal gyroscope that I had always trusted and depended on instantly made a hundred and eighty degree correction. I was right back where I had started!

My brain commanded my body to move the very second the error was discovered. I turned around without question or hesitation and stepped off back down the road in the direction from which I had just come. I didn't take more than three or four steps before I stopped again. Hadn't I decided earlier that leaving the old man was a mistake?

'Maybe,' part of me conceded, 'but it's too late to change your mind now. Something about that old man wasn't right. Get going.'

I took another hesitant step before stopping again. What was it about Mart that wasn't right? The old man didn't know me from Adam and yet he still treated me better than my own father ever had.

'And why do you suppose he did that?' my jaded side countered. 'You know the old guy is after something; you just don't know what it is yet. You might think he's a nice guy right now but there's going to be a catch somewhere along the line... there always is. Somewhere down the road you're going to get hurt. You'd be better off to cut your losses now and keep going.'

My body took another involuntary step before I could stop it. Clenching my teeth, I set my suitcase down, opened it and fished out my smokes. Something was wrong with my inured reasoning- there had to be. Was it that impossible to believe that the old man might want to help me for the simple reason that he was just a nice guy? Hadn't I ever helped anyone without expecting something in return? What about Cindy? Hadn't I left without a word of complaint when she asked me to? Irritated with the conflict raging in my head, I lit my cigarette, tossed the match and smoked as I paced back and forth in the dark.

All my life I had followed my instincts without question and, as far as I could tell, they had never steered me wrong. Why was I so tempted to ignore them now? I had already walked away from the old man and his help, going back on that or any other decision I had made was just something I didn't do. Once my mind was made up I always stuck with it, come hell or high water. It hadn't always been the easiest thing to do sometimes, but then again, I never really felt like I had a choice before.

"God works in mysterious ways."

Mom's disjointed voice whispered in my head and added to the debate. Anxious to find a legitimate excuse for changing my mind, I stopped pacing and considered the God angle in this mess that was my life.

Part of me desperately wanted to argue the point that God didn't even exist but the argument was cut off at the knees as I remembered what Mart had said about his promising God he'd help any kid who needed it and how he didn't think I had any say in how I ended up in his driveway.

God works in mysterious ways.

I shook my head and tried to think.

It had been easy for me to just write Mart's words off as coincidence or lies and call it good the first time I had heard them, but now- after walking four or five hours in what I had thought was the opposite direction only to end up right back where I had started- I had to wonder if maybe the old man wasn't a little closer to the truth than I gave him credit for. While I might have just had my brains scrambled a bit, I knew I had started walking in the direction of Grand Rapids after Bowl Head and his cronies drove away...or at least I thought I knew. Either way, I did know for a fact that I wasn't standing in front of Mart's house again through any conscious decision on my part, and now that I was, writing the whole deal off as sheer coincidence was a whole lot harder to do and I was far too tired and confused to make the effort.

Tossing my smoke into the ditch, I grabbed my suitcase before I could change my mind and started up the driveway toward the house.

I must have been about ten feet away from reaching Mart's pickup when I heard the familiar 'chink' of a Zippo. My heart lurched in my chest at the unexpected noise and I stopped dead in my tracks. There was a quick scraping sound, a small 'whoooph' and a yellow flame flared up, casting a flickering glow over the old man's neck and face. He was sitting in a lawn chair next his battered black truck, opposite the house. Taking his time, he slowly raised the Zippo and lit a cigarette before snapping the lid back down and killing the flame. I took a deep breath and walked toward the small glowing coal that marked the end of Mart's smoke. By the time I drew even with the back of his truck I was able to see him pretty well.

Tucking the cigarette in his mouth, the old man reached over and picked up another folded lawn chair he had leaning up against his truck. Shaking it open, he set the chair up on the gravel next to his. I set my suitcase down between the two chairs and sat down. Now that I knew I didn't have any farther to walk, I was suddenly dead on my feet. I leaned back in the chair and my eyes immediately slid closed of their own accord.

"I was pulling for you out there, son." Mart's quiet voice was solemn.

I opened my eyes, looked over at the old man and then out at the road. I was surprised to see that I could make out the now familiar shape of his rusty mailbox.

"You were watching me?" I asked evenly.

"I was," he nodded, looking off in the distance. "You weren't much more than a restless shadow blowing around out there but I could see you."

I found the thought of Mart watching me without me knowing it to be kind of spooky and more than a little embarrassing. I wanted to be angry but after remembering the way I had left him earlier that night, I quickly realized I didn't have reason nor the strength to pull it off.

"Why didn't you say anything?" I asked.

Mart crossed his legs, looked down at his cigarette and tapped the ash.

"Oh, I said something," he nodded. Taking a drag off his smoke, he glanced over at me and smiled. "I just didn't say it to you."

Mart and I looked at each other for a second or two but I found I didn't have anything to say. Mart quietly nodded the subject closed and looked away to the black horizon. The two of us sat silently for a while and took in the night. The overwhelming quietness, so foreign to me just hours earlier, was now inexplicably comforting somehow. Creatures of the night chirped and called and vibrated back and forth around us, chasing and feeding and searching for mates, but these sounds were as much a part of the night as the darkness that defined it or the stars and the moon that illuminated it; they belonged there.

My body hummed with fatigue and my thoughts were slow and thick. God, I was tired. My eyes slid closed and everything came rushing back- the word Greyhound printed in the shape of a bus across the top of the piece of paper propped against my cereal bowl, the nervous butterflies of dread fluttering around in my gut as I read the words Trufant, Michigan written in pen above the mechanically printed word Destination. I remembered the bus ride; the numberless, diesel smelling stops along the way, the slimy, metallic taste of stolen cold Spam and the tired beaten looks of the other riders. 'What's your name, asshole?' Jim asked. 'I'm sorry, Kenny, you aren't going to be able to stay here,' Cindy cried. 'What are you doing out here, kid?'

I was walking. A car was coming up behind me- a Michigan State Police car- but I couldn't stop walking. I wanted to step into the ditch- I had to step into the ditch; that's what I did when I heard the car coming up behind me. There were two cops riding inside the car, one of them was talking to the other and they weren't going to see me because I was going to step into the ditch and stop walking so they could drive by...only I wasn't going to stop this time. I had to keep walking. Over and over, one foot in front of the-

I woke up with a violent start that rattled my cheap lawn chair as needless adrenaline coursed through my body.

My throat and ears throbbed in time with the freewheel pumping of my heart and my eyes darted around the darkness of Mart's yard in a blind panic. My head felt prickly and brittle and, even though I already knew I had been dreaming, I was scared.

"Hell of a way to wake up, eh?"

I jumped a little at Mart's voice and gave him a confused look. "Oh, man," I said, sitting up in my chair. "How long was I asleep?"

"Minute, maybe two." Mart dropped his cigarette to the ground between his feet and squashed it out with his toe. "Used to do that myself, wake up like you just did. Used to scare the hell out of Mary too, let me tell you. I'd just start to drop off and all of a sudden I'd be back straddling that damn Deere, plowing the same fields I'd just spent the last two days on...only I'd be plowing crossways against the rows I'd already seeded... or the steering wheel would come off in my hands and there wouldn't be any brakes. I don't know; something always went wrong and when it did I'd jump awake like a man peeing on an electric fence."

I didn't say anything; the burst of adrenaline was gone and I was beginning to feel decidedly punky. I didn't have anything left; I had gone too far on too little and lost too much along the way. The very thought of trying to carry on a conversation was exhausting. All I wanted to do was to go inside, lie down on Mart's couch and go to sleep for about a week. I just couldn't figure out how to ask.

"You hungry, boy?" Mart asked. "I drove uptown and picked up a couple things after you left."

"No, sir," I answered. "I guess I'd just like to go lie down on your couch if it's alright with you."

"Door's open," he said without moving. "Go on in and make yourself at home. You'll find some bed linens set out on the couch, though I doubt you'll be needing the blanket. I'll be in directly."

Relieved, I started to push myself up out of my chair

but stopped as something occurred to me.

"Why did you do that?" I asked. Mart gave me a quizzical look. "Why did you set bed linens out on the couch? And the food; why did you go into town and buy food after I left?"

Mart looked back out toward the road and considered the question as he pulled out another cigarette and lit up.

"I was hoping you'd come back," he said, glancing over at me. "I sure wasn't expecting you to... but I was hoping."

"Oh," I said. I couldn't understand why Mart gave a rat's ass what happened to me- I sure wasn't anyone to him- but it really didn't matter anyway; I couldn't have walked any further that night even if I had wanted to. I got up from my chair and picked up my suitcase.

"Thanks," I said. Mart nodded.

"Good night, boy," he said.

I turned and walked into the house.

It was the birds that woke me up the next morning...the birds and the curtains.

According to the clock setting on the TV it was 9:15; the day was already warm and an even coat of sweat covered my body. The two windows I could see from the couch without moving my head were open; long gauzy brown curtains snapped and billowed on the crest of the hot summer breeze passing through the screens. The birds outside sounded hurried and determined, almost impatient, their calls quick and loud. The waving curtains were comfortable to watch, nearly hypnotizing. I wasn't sure where I was but I was awake enough to sense that watching the weightless rise and fall of curtains in the wind wasn't such a bad place to be. It didn't last long, this suspended state of awareness, a minute, maybe two, but it was nice while it lasted.

Sitting up on the couch, I caught a movement out of the corner of my eye. Turning my head quickly to get a better look, I saw a monochromatic reflection of myself inside the screen of the television set across the room. I raised my hand and watched as the smaller version of myself did the same. I tried looking at his/my face but the light was wrong, the reflection too muddy and small. I didn't like that. I wasn't sure why I didn't like it (Is that really me?) but I wasn't interested in thinking about it; I just looked away at the first tickle in my gut.

I glanced over at Mart's easy chair next to the couch and jumped a little at the sight of him reclined there, sleeping. The old man's feet were bare and he was wearing a sleeveless white t-shirt and the same polyester slacks from the day before. As if sensing my stare, he snorted softly and turned his head a little to one side. Not wanting to wake the man, I quietly collected my clothes and padded out to the kitchen where I quickly got dressed. Remembering what he had said about picking up some food the day before, I checked out the refrigerator as soon as I had finished.

Easing the refrigerator door open, I was immediately rewarded with the sight of a six pack of Coca-Cola. While I was actually more of a Mountain Dew man, a can of pop- any pop- was still kind of a special occasion for me.

Besides the Coke, the old man had bought a gallon of milk, a loaf of white bread, a dozen eggs, and a combination package of four different kinds of sliced lunchmeats; ham, salami, bologna, and something called olive loaf. Seeing that the package had already been opened, I grabbed a couple slices of bologna, pulled a Coke from the six pack and closed the refrigerator door. I started to pull the ring tab on my Coke but thought better of it; I didn't know if Mart was a sound sleeper or not and I wanted a little time to think things through before he got up. Stepping outside, I sat down on the porch steps and started in on my breakfast.

Due to the recuperating powers known only to the young, my body felt pretty good. I still had a nasty knot on my head and my hands were both swollen and stiff, but those were things I could see and feel and it was obvious they weren't serious; they would heal.

As tired as I had been the night before, I laid awake for the better part of an hour after getting settled on Mart's couch... my brain just refused to shut down. I studied my situation seven ways from Sunday but I kept coming to the same conclusion; I had to get back to California somehow and find my dad...but I had to do it right; I knew my chances of being welcomed back with open arms were slim to none if I showed up on his doorstep hungry and broke. Oh, I didn't think he'd send me packing right off the bat or anything like that but I didn't have any doubts that my stay would be temporary and brief. The way I saw it, the odds of dad letting me stay with him and Sheila would jump dramatically if I were to knock on his door with no postage due and a few extra dollars in my pocket besides- just to grease the rails a bit, if you know what I mean. All I had to do was figure out how to come up with the money.

"Still here, eh?"

I jumped a little at Mart's voice behind me. Swiveling around on my step I saw he was standing inside the house on the other side of the screen door.

"Yes, sir," I said, squinting against the sun. "I grabbed a Coke and some bologna, I hope that was alright."

"That's what it's there for," he nodded absently, looking out through the screen to his weed infested yard. Pushing the door open, he stepped outside and walked across the porch to stand at the rail next to the steps. He didn't look too good; kind of bristly and a little lost, like he hadn't gotten a whole lot of sleep. Throw in a healthy case of the shakes and he'd have looked exactly like my dad after a three day bender. I popped the last crescent piece of bologna into my mouth and chased it down with a healthy slug of pop. Out in the yard the wind picked up a notch and the weeds bobbed and bent in gently traveling waves.

"Well, what are your plans for today, boy?" he asked. "Think you'll be around for supper?"

I glanced up but the old man was staring off in the direction of his weather beaten barn. Take all the time you want, I'll wait. I pulled out my matches and an after breakfast cigarette. The wind blew out the first match before I could get it up to my cigarette. I tried another but the wind killed that one too. Mart silently fished his Zippo out of his pant's pocket and started to hand it to me.

"What the hell happened to you?"

The Zippo in his hand forgotten, Mart took a half step toward me, studying the side of my face. I knew it looked pretty ugly, I had checked it out in the bathroom mirror the night before and had been kind of shocked myself. The knot on my head from slamming into the pavement was hidden up under my hair but the whole right side of my face was a hideous shade of yellowish purple and my eye was nearly swollen shut. It didn't really hurt but it sure looked like hell.

"I got in a fight," I said, still holding my hand out for the lighter. "It's not as bad as it looks."

Grimacing, the old man reached out and started to push my hair up back with his thumb.

"I'm alright," I said, pulling my head back. I didn't mean to be disrespectful; it was just something I did without thinking. Mart pulled back a little and studied me mildly.

"Can I use your lighter for a second," I said, trying to sound apologetic. The old man held his gaze for a second before handing it over.

"You're not much of a talker are you, boy?" he said as I worked the lighter. I glanced up from my cigarette and saw he was staring at the barked up knuckles on my Zippo holding hand.

"I guess not," I admitted. I snapped the lighter closed and handed it back. I was still worried about appearing rude so I went on. "My dad used to tell people I wouldn't say shit if I had a mouthful."

"Well, I can believe that," Mart said quietly. Slipping the lighter back into his pocket, he rested his arms on the porch rail and went back to staring off at the barn. The ball was back in my court. I thought for a minute while I smoked.

"I'd like to stay here for another day or two," I started, "but I've got to earn some money somehow. I was wondering if you could hire me to do some work for you, maybe mow your lawn or something like that."

Mart stood silent and, for a while, we both watched the wind and the birds.

"How much money do you need, boy?" he finally asked.

"About forty dollars."

I was actually hoping to earn at least fifty but even forty dollars was a huge chunk of change in '74 and, while it had seemed a reasonable enough amount the night before, it now sounded almost ludicrous in the harsh light of day. What the hell had I been thinking?

The old man lifted his head and scratched at the underside of his whisker-shadowed chin.

"Scoot on over there." He motioned me over to one side of the porch stairway with a wave of his hand. Picking up my pop, I moved over and Mart sat down on the step next to me. The old man paused for a second, glanced at me and then reached around to pull a worn black wallet from his back pocket. Opening it with one practiced hand, he fished around inside with the other and carefully pulled out a folded piece of paper. Holding the paper in his left hand, he sat up and put the wallet back in his pocket.

"I found this on my sixtieth birthday; April seventh, nineteen hundred and fifty-two." he said, deftly coaxing the folded paper apart with his blunt and clumsy looking thumbs. I did some quick mental math and discovered Mart was eighty-two years old! I was shocked. To a fourteen-year-old, forty was pretty damn old; eighty-two wasn't even conceivable.

Shocked as I was, the old man's age was promptly forgotten when, for the first time in my life, I found myself looking at an honest to God one hundred dollar bill in Mart's fingers... a see-though thin hundred dollar bill, one divided into four sections by three permanent creases, but a hundred dollar bill just the same.

"Wow," I said reverently. "Where'd you find it?"

"Sticking out of a mostly melted snowdrift in the

back forty. Mary and I were out loading up a wagon of winter rocks when I heard it fluttering in the wind. How it ever ended up out in that field I'll never know- the nearest house besides ours was better than two miles away back then- but that's where it was and that's where I found it."

"Oh man," I said, staring at the bill. I had found a crumpled one dollar bill on the sidewalk once and I remembered feeling like I was one of the luckiest people on the planet; I walked into the first gas station I came to and bought two packs of cigarettes and four Slim Jims...

I turned and looked at Mart incredulously.

"Why didn't you spend it?" I asked. Saving money, especially found money, was never a strong suit in the Malone family.

"Wasn't mine," Mart said simply, "at least not at first. A hundred dollars was worth a whole lot more back then than it is now and I was sure whoever lost it would turn up sooner or later. I spread the word around town that I had found something but no one ever stepped up to say they had lost anything other than one of the Streeter boys asking about a goat. Mary and I weren't wanting for anything at the time so I just ended up hanging on to it."

The old man paused for a second and then suddenly tugged at the opposite ends of the bill, pulling it in half. The bill was so worn and the center crease so deep it didn't even make a ripping sound; it separated with a soft 'pop'. I looked up at Mart in shock.

"Here," he said, holding out the half in his left hand. "I want you have this." I looked from Mart to the bill back to Mart again. "Go on," he nodded. "Take it."

Taking the torn bill from his fingers, I slowly turned it over and examined both sides.

"Is this real?" I asked suspiciously.

"It is," Mart nodded. "Or at least as far as I know it is. And I've got to believe the chances of finding a counterfeit hundred dollar bill out in my back forty are even slimmer than finding the real McCoy."

I didn't get it. I had read somewhere that you could turn torn bills in at any bank and they would give you a whole one in exchange, but the catch was you had to have more than half the bill... Mart had torn this one right down the middle; one half wasn't worth squat without the other.

"Why are you giving me this?" I asked. Mart didn't answer right away; his eyes roamed across the yard as he pulled out a cigarette, tapped it on his wrist a couple of times and lit up.

"I want to help you, boy," he said slowly, stopping to pluck a stray piece of tobacco off his lower lip, "but I'm afraid I might not be the best man for the job. I don't have the foggiest idea what to do for you. Mary would have known. You never would have walked away from this house yesterday had Mary been sitting at the table with us. Why, she'd have sent me off to go peddle my papers right out of the gate and you'd have ended up telling her your whole life story over a glass of milk and a plate of fresh baked snickerdoodles... but Mary's gone now and I'm afraid I've never been much of a cook.

"I'm sixty-eight years older than you are, son...I thought helping you would be easy. I've got a lifetime of experience beyond your fourteen years but it's a lifetime that was spent right here on this farm; the only things I know are the things I had to know to provide for my family. I can tell when it's time to sweeten the soil with a crop of beans just by the way the dirt smells after a spring rain. I know how to birth a breached calf without killing the mother and I guess I can fix damn near anything you've got that runs on gas and oil... but I'm afraid I don't know much when it comes to fixing people; that was always Mary's job."

The old man pushed himself up and walked down to stand at the base of the stairs. He stood there with his back to me for maybe a minute- looking at nothing in particular that I could see- before turning around.

"If money is all you need from me, that's fine," Mart held out his half of the hundred-dollar bill. "You say the word and I'll hand this over. We'll go inside, tape it back together and you can be on your way."

Dumbfounded, I blinked at Mart's half of the bill as I tried to make sense out of what he was telling me. My heart was galloping along at the thought of having a hundred dollars all to myself but another part of me held back, unconvinced.

"Oh, come on," I said suspiciously. "What's the catch?"

"The fact that you have to ask me for this half *is* the catch," he said. "*When* you ask me for it is completely up to you. I guess it might be a cowardly way of doing things but I'm just too damn old to live with any more regrets than I already have. I'll do whatever I can for you, son, but I'm afraid you're the one that's going to have to decide what it is that needs doing. All I'm going to say is this: I'm not so sure money is the answer to your problems. I don't know what you've got waiting for you down the road but I suspect it's nothing that can't wait and you're more than welcome to stay here for as long as you want. I'll tell you, son; I think you could do a lot worse than spending a few days right here."

I don't know what you've got waiting for you down the road... I stared at the worn piece of paper in Mart's hand as his words repeated in my head. What did I have waiting for me down the road? Dear old dad hadn't sent me three thousand miles away out of the goodness of his heart; he'd sent me here because he wanted me gone- and you couldn't get much more gone than Sticksville, Michigan. And while I'd gladly ride a Greyhound twenty-four hours a day for the next five years if it could take me back to my mom, the thought of riding that damn bus for another five barren days just to get back to dad and Sheila was about as appealing as walking back...or maybe even a little less so. Walking back would take a lot longer than five days and, now that I had a reason to think about it, I wasn't in any rush to get back.

It suddenly occurred to me that one of the most appealing aspects of my plan to get back to California was the fact that it would have taken me days or even weeks to earn enough money to start back. Now with Mart offering me more than enough money to cover the trip, that buffer of time was gone and I could see my plan for what it was; a fourteen-year-old boy's game of make believe. Living with dad and Sheila had sucked before I left and there wasn't a chance in hell it was going to be any better after I got back. Like Mart said, I could do a lot worse than spending a few days here...and that was really kind of sad when you thought about it for a minute.

"How long do you think it would take me to mow your lawn?" I asked. If the old man was serious about giving me a hundred dollars, and I was pretty sure he was, I figured the least I could do was help him out with a few chores before I left. Mart looked at me for a second or two before turning to survey his overgrown yard.

"Oh, a day, maybe two," he said. "And it'd be a hell of a job, too; I guess I pretty much let the whole place go to pot since I lost Mary. Weeds would all have to be scythed down and hauled off before a man could even think about cranking up the lawnmower."

"What's a scythe?" I asked.

Mart turned and looked at me like he thought I was pulling his leg. After seeing that I wasn't, he smiled quietly.

"Tell you what," he said, taking one last drag off his smoke before dropping it at his feet and toeing it out. "I'm going back inside to get a little more sleep. Why don't you take yourself a trip out to the barn and do a little exploring. You're not expected to do a damn thing around here but if you really think you want to work on the yard you'll find the scythe hanging in the crib with the rakes and shovels. The lawnmower is right there too but like I said, you won't be needing that for a while."

"Okay," I said, standing up. "Do I need a key?"

"How's that?" Mart gave me a strange look. "A key? A key for what?"

"The barn," I said. "Don't you keep your barn locked up?" I thought I saw a twinkle of a smile in Mart's eyes but to his credit the old man managed to keep a straight face.

"Can't say as I ever had any call to lock up my barn." The old man pulled out a calico handkerchief and gave his nose a couple dry perfunctory honks before folding it up and slipping it back into his pocket.

"Oh," I said. I stood there awkwardly for a second before starting down the steps.

"Now mind what I said, boy." Mart stopped me with a finger on my shoulder. "You don't have to lift a finger around here unless you've a mind to, you hear?"

"Yes sir," I nodded. "I understand."

"All right then." Satisfied, Mart dropped his hand and gave me a nod. I started for the barn again but hadn't taken more than four or five steps before Mart stopped me once more.

"Hey, boy," he called. I stopped and turned around. The old man was tapping another cigarette on his wrist.

"You ever gone fishing?" he asked.

"Fishing?" I knew what fishing was- Huckleberry Finn was one of my favorite books of all time- but that was about it.

"No sir," I answered.

Mart paused as he was bringing his Zippo up to his smoke and looked at me. Finally, with an almost imperceptible shake of his head, he lit his cigarette and snapped the lighter closed. Giving me a little wave, he turned and started up the stairs. I watched and waited until the screen door slammed behind him before I turned and started off again.

The walk out to the barn turned out to be a lot harder than it looked. Blazing my way through the thigh-high weeds and scrub brush that had taken over Mart's backyard was no picnic in itself, but the yard only stretched back a hundred foot or so from the house; the remaining two or three hundred yards between the yard and the barn was a jungle thicket of saplings, thorn bushes, and a bunch of tall grabby blades of some mutant strain of sharp, thin grass. Making my way through that crap was a real chore. By the time I made it up the gentle earthen slope to the barn's two huge hanging doors I was hot, sweaty, and bleeding from a bunch of different thorn punctures and grass cuts. Stepping out of the brush onto a short, two-foot cement ramp leading up to the doors, I tilted my head back and tried to catch my breath.

The barn was huge. Breathing hard, I took a dizzy step back to try and get some perspective on the size of the thing but it was no good; from where I was standing the sun bleached boards seemed to stretch up to the sky. A few wispy clouds were floating by and I had to look down as they suddenly seemed to stop in mid air and the barn wall appeared to move.

It didn't take me long to figure out how the twin doors were suppose to work but getting them to work was another story. Each door hung from two stout but rusted iron wheels that in turn rested on a rail attached to the barn wall. In theory, all I had to do was slip my hand through a worn hole in either door and slide it away from the other, but, since Mart evidently hadn't made the trip out to his barn since he last mowed his grass, the bearings in the wheels that the heavy doors hung from were rusted tight. Ten minutes of grunting, pulling, and more sweating rewarded me with an open space of about six inches between the doors- just wide enough to slip through but only after I got down on my hands and knees and wedged the bottom of the right door away from the barn with my shoulder. As I squeezed my way in, the door flopped back against the barn wall and there was a sudden soft explosion of frantic pigeon wings as four or five of the birds short hopped it back and forth between the rafters high above my head. Ignoring them (the sound of pigeons was as familiar to me as the sound of my own voice), I stood up and blinked in the relative darkness of the barn and waited for my eyes to adjust. It didn't take long.

The interior of the massive structure was illuminated by dusty shafts of sunlight streaming through irregular gaps in the wide, rough-cut boards that made up the exterior walls. The air was surprisingly cool compared to the growing heat outside and the smell of the place was of things old and forgotten: sweet moldy hay, dry cracked leather, old wood, and time. The skeleton of the building- long telephone pole size logs hand hewed into square beams- loomed above me, while the floor- thick, two foot wide slabs of virgin pine, Mart would later tell me- felt as firm as the earth itself. I had the strangest feeling that I had just returned to a comfortable, familiar place I had known and loved sometime in my past.

I couldn't get enough of the place; I started off looking for Mart's lawn tools but I couldn't find them or anything that looked like a 'crib' and I soon lost all track of time as I wandered around looking at the strange variety of items that had somehow found their way inside the old barn. I touched an ancient, deflated punching bag and wondered who had hung it and whose fist had punched it last. I climbed in and sat down on the horsehair (and pigeon shit) - covered cushion of a horse drawn snow sleigh that could have been the model for a Currier and Ives Christmas postcard. I held the detached earpiece of a wooden, hand crank box phone to my ear and gave the crank a careful turn. I picked up and dropped an airless, mushroom shaped basketball to see if it would bounce (it didn't), and, after figuring out that it was dead, I marveled and then mourned over the dried out and remarkably preserved corpse of a long dead raccoon. The raccoon held my attention for a while. It wasn't stuffed; it had died right where I found it. The way he died still haunts me to this day.

I found the raccoon over in the darkest corner of the barn after pushing a baby carriage back and forth to see if the wheels still turned. They turned all right but the front end of the thing popped up as the tires rolled up and over something. Curious, I pulled the carriage back to see what the wheels were hitting and just about jumped out of my skin at the sight of a bushy, ringed tail attached to a mound of brown and tan animal fur. While it only took a second to know that the animal was dead, all I could see was the back end of it and I wasn't sure what kind of animal it was. Being a boy, I was naturally curious. Picking up a thin, hollow curtain rod from a bunch leaning against the wall, I gently pushed at the unidentified animal, trying to turn it around so I could see the head. The body was light (the worms and bugs had finished their work years earlier, glimpses of bare white bone showed through a few elongated holes in the stiff hide) but it didn't want to move. The back end was loose, it lifted easily when I slid the rod up under the hindquarters, but something seemed to be holding the head firmly in place. Had I been a year or two older I would have lost interest at that point and moved on, a year or two younger and I'd have been too nervous to try and identify it in the first place. Unfortunately I wasn't either of those. I was fourteen and I had to know. Bracing myself with a hand against the back wall, I leaned over the dead animal's eviscerated body and took a look. I saw what I saw and, after realizing what it meant, I mourned the animal's fate.

I don't know why the raccoon went inside the barn in the first place but I do know when: just before Mart rolled the big twin doors closed for the last time. The barn was evidently well built, the only way out for an animal that size was the way he had gotten in... but the doors were far too big and heavy for him to move. He was trapped.

In my mind I can still see the raccoon shuffling around the building looking for an opening, getting thirstier and hungrier as the minutes stretched into hours and the hours to days. How long could he have stayed alive? Three days? Four? Ten? Raccoons are natural climbers; did he notice the pigeons? Did he scale the lofty heights of the rafters and prolong his agony by eating their eggs? How many times did he stick his paw out through the odd knothole in the walls, blindly groping in the fresh pure air outside in the vain hope of finding food or water?

Eventually the raccoon found the spot where he ultimately died. It was a hole in the floor. Not a very big hole but one he probably could have squeezed through had he had the chance. In a grim, ironic twist of fate worthy of Hawthorne (or more likely King, now that I think about it), a heavy piece of thick wire screen had been nailed over the opening to keep animals like the raccoon out. The raccoon died here, looking down through this screen; his paws were still gripping the wire mesh, the clean empty sockets where his eyes had once been still staring down at the hope of a rectangular patch of sunlight on the dirt floor below.

I went numb. The realization of the suffering the poor simple animal had experienced before he died overloaded the already straining circuit board of my soul and tripped a safety breaker... but in the second before that breaker let go, I caught a glimpse of something, a wisp of dark knowledge that no fourteen year-old boy had a right to even recognize, let alone understand, and it scared me to the core even as I acknowledged its possibilities.

The raccoon had gone through hell before he died but that was all behind him now; his troubles on this earth were over.

I pushed myself back up away from the wall, turned

and walked away. I knew now that there was a lower level below the floor I was standing on; Mart's tools had to be down there and I had to go find a way to get in. I shimmed my way back out between the doors and started looking.

“HEY BOY!”

I looked up from swinging the scythe and saw Mart standing on the porch.

“LET’S EAT!” he called.

I acknowledged the man with a wave and he went back inside. Running my hand back through my sweat drenched hair, I turned around to survey my progress.

Finding my way into the lower level of the barn had been surprisingly easy. Rather than fighting my way back down the slope that had brought me up to the barn’s twin doors, I decided to stick to the edge of the building and make my way around its perimeter. I hadn’t walked but ten feet or so before finding myself standing on top of one of the slope’s rock foundation walls. The door to the lower level was below me and about three or four feet away- a horseshoe nailed above the door was about level with my feet. I climbed down the wall, fought my way over to the door (a conventional, albeit homemade, hinged type of door this time with a wooden latch rather than a doorknob) and pushed it open.

Stepping into the lower level of Mart’s barn was like walking into an abandoned, tornado-ravaged museum. There was crap everywhere (two things in particular- a yellow snowmobile and a canvas tarp covered car- would have grabbed my interest immediately had I started on this level rather than one above it) but I didn’t give any of it any more than a cursory glance; I had already done more than my share of exploring for the day.

I found Mart’s tools in a room that looked like it had

been built down there as an afterthought. Using the process of elimination I figured out which long handled tool inside was a scythe, took it down from the nail it was hanging from and headed back outside. I was in and out in a minute or less and the fact that most of the seven or eight windows I saw down there either had broken panes or no glass at all barely registered with me.

Knowing I was going to have to get the lawnmower out of the barn and up to the yard sooner or later, I started swinging the scythe with my first step out the door. I hadn't made it more than a hundred feet or so before the first blisters started forming on the palms of my hands. By the time I reached the yard, a lot of them had popped and the scythe handle was wet and slippery from their weeping. Other than the ten seconds or so it took me to peel my t-shirt off and hang it on a bush, I never stopped swinging. I might have slowed down quite a bit from my original pace but I never stopped.

Now, leaning on the scythe and surveying how much ground I had cleared, I was pleasantly surprised at the dent I had made in the job. The trail I had whacked down from the barn to the yard wasn't exactly straight (it's hard to tell where you're headed when the weeds are taller than you are) but walking back out there next time was going to be an easy stroll down a flat, four foot wide path. And besides that, I'd managed to clear most of a ten-foot wide strip that ran along the whole length of the back yard. I was hot, exhausted, and my blistered hands hurt like hell but my mind had a fresh, washed out feeling and that alone made it all worthwhile. I took a lot of pleasure in walking over the thick carpet of chopped weeds on my way out to retrieve my shirt.

Lunch was a scant affair consisting of white bread stacked on a plate, the plastic package of lunchmeats I had raided for breakfast, and the jar of pickles left over from the sixties. I ate four sandwiches (two bologna, one ham, and one salami... I just didn't like the look of that olive loaf), drank two glasses of milk and a can of Coke and steered clear of the pickles all together. Mart didn't have anything at all except for a cup of coffee but I didn't really take any notice; I just figured he had already eaten.

"You're kind of rough on your hands, aren't you boy," Mart said as I swallowed the last bite of my fourth sandwich.

"Oh, they're okay," I said, looking at my blistered palms.

The old man squashed his cigarette out in the ashtray, stood up and walked out into the mudroom. Pulling out my matches and a cigarette, I turned in my chair and watched as he opened up a closet door and rummaged around inside. Not wanting to appear nosy I turned back to the table and lit up.

"Here you go." Mart set a pair of stained, tan leathers gloves on the table next to me and sat back down. "Had I been thinking I'd have given you those earlier. No sense in blistering up your mitts if you don't have to."

"Thank you," I said, picking up the gloves. "I appreciate it." I pushed my chair back and started to get up.

"Now hang on there a second, boy," Mart said. "Where you going?"

"Back to work," I said. I liked the way that sounded when I said it. Back to work. It made me feel older, kind of confident and self-sufficient.

"Oh, hell," Mart said. "Those weeds aren't going anywhere. Sit down for a minute, I want to talk to you."

I settled back down on my chair and looked around the room, feeling nervous. I figured the old man was going to ask me about how I'd come to end up so far from home and I wasn't sure yet how I wanted to answer that question. After Mart let a silent minute or so slide by without saying anything, I guess I panicked.

"I can cook, you know," I blurted out.

"Is that right?" The old man looked relieved and the tone of his voice was a tad too enthusiastic. I suddenly realized the old man was just as nervous as I was. While I couldn't understand how an eighty-two-year old man could feel nervous about talking to a kid like me, I found the knowledge reassuring somehow.

"Yes sir," I went on. "Hamburgers, hot dogs, and macaroni and cheese, mostly, but if you wanted to pick up some stuff like that next time you go to the store I'd pay for my half after we turn that hundred dollar bill into the bank. It'd save you some money, I think."

"Well, I guess that sounds like a deal," Mart nodded. "But there's no call for you to worry about paying me back. I'm not a rich man but I'm not exactly hurting either. We'll just count your cooking as half and call it good."

The two of us lapsed into silence again but this time it was a little more comfortable, at least for me. I considered trying to make some more small talk but decided against it. The old man had something he wanted to say and, even though I didn't know him very well, I had a pretty good idea that my putting it off by talking about the weather or something lame like that wasn't going to change his mind.

"Listen boy," he finally said, pulling out a cigarette. "You and I have got something that we've got to clear up."

"All right," I said, shifting in my chair. Ready or not, here it comes.

"Now, I don't know anything about you, son," he started carefully, "and that's okay, I'm not asking any questions here- but I know I said something yesterday to get your fur up, something that pushed you out that door and down the road, but I'll be damned if I can figure out what it was."

"Oh, that was just-" I stopped as Mart held up his hand.

"Now hear me out," he said. "I've got more respect than you'll ever know for a man who listens more than he talks and I don't know that I've ever met anyone better at it than you. I'm not looking for any explanations here; I'm just looking for a little leeway... a little piece of mind."

"I guess I don't know what you mean," I said tentatively.

"What I mean is this;" he said as he lit his smoke, "I don't want to have to worry about stepping on your toes every time I say something around you. It seems you've got a bit of a hair trigger when it comes to things you feel strongly about but there's no way for me to know what those things are, you see?" Mart paused. Reaching across the table, he pulled the ashtray over to his side.

"Now I'm not much of a talker myself," he said, tapping his ash, "but I don't want to have to try and walk on eggshells without breaking them every time I open my mouth around you. Maybe in the next couple of days you'll see your way clear to tell me how you ended up in this neck of the woods, but until that day comes- if it ever does at all- I'm hoping you'll have a little patience and try to see things from my point of view. How about it, is that a deal?"

I couldn't believe what I was hearing. I wasn't anybody to this old man, yet here he was asking me to have patience with him! Unbelievable.

"It's a deal," I said.

Mart held his hand out to me across the table and we shook on it.

"All right then," he said, taking his hand back, "Now that we've got that settled, I'm going to run on into Greenville this afternoon, you want to ride along?"

"Greenville?" I said. "Where's that?"

"Oh, 12, 13 miles from here, I guess," he said. "Won't take but an hour or two."

"I don't think so," I answered. I assumed the old man was asking just to be polite and besides, I'd done enough riding over the last week to last me quite a while. I liked the idea of not having to go anywhere, even if it was only for a day or two.

"Suit yourself." Mart sounded pleasant enough but it was obvious he was disappointed that I didn't want to go.

"You need me to bring you back anything?" he asked.

"Well," I said hesitantly. "I guess I could use another pack of Marlboros."

Actually I needed quite a few things, not the least of which was a toothbrush, but I couldn't bring myself to ask the old man for more than what he was already doing for me. At fourteen, I had only set one real goal for my life and that goal was to not end up like my dad; I wasn't ever going to drink and I would never allow myself to take advantage of anyone. I wouldn't even have asked Mart for the smokes but I knew myself well enough to know I'd be walking the ditches looking for returnable bottles in about four hours or so if I didn't ask for them now.

Mart studied me silently. I knew what he was thinking- he had seen what I was carrying in my suitcase- but telling him why I couldn't ask for anything would have meant talking about my dad and I wasn't ready to do that.

"You sure, boy?" he asked.

"Yes sir," I said, looking him in the eye. The old man held my gaze for a second before shifting in his chair and adjusting the position of the ashtray on the table.

"Listen son," he said, looking back up at me. "I plan on paying you twenty-five cents an hour for the time you spend working out in the yard."

"But..." I started to protest.

"Now you just simmer down there, Skippy," he interrupted sharply. "Give me a chance to finish here and then I'll listen to you, okay?"

"All right," I said, setting back. I'd listen but I wasn't about to separate the old man from any more of his money. I was looking for ways to balance the scales a little; letting Mart pay me for working on his yard would only make that harder to do.

"I told you this morning you weren't expected to lift a finger around here and I meant it," he said. "You ain't nothing but skin and bones, your eyes look like two pee holes in deep snow, and if you ask me, the side of your face that's not all beat to hell looks a might peaked. You ought to be in bed- hell, you probably ought to be in the hospital, for that matter- but not you. You're out there in the sun working on the worst looking yard this side of the Mackinaw Bridge and you're doing it without a word of complaint. You are something special, son, and I don't think you really know it. Oh, I think you know you're smarter than the average bear, you're too quiet and you think too much to not know that, but it takes someone special to do more than what's asked of him just because it's the right thing to do, and for doing that I'm paying you a quarter an hour for your time. It isn't much but I kinda figured you'd have a problem with taking anything more from me so I sat down and worked it out. You might be getting room and board here but the way I look at it, twenty-five cents an hour is at least a dollar an hour less than what I'd have to pay some Joe Blow down the street to scythe and mow this yard- and I can guarantee he wouldn't work half as hard as you have been. So if you think about it you'll be paying me a dollar for every hour I'm paying you a quarter. Now you've worked what so far, four hours today?"

"Don't know," I shrugged. "I wasn't keeping track."

"Well, let's call it four for right now. At a quarter an hour that means I owe you a buck but I've actually made four. I don't care how you cut it, I'm coming out on the winning end of this deal."

"Except you'd never have hired anyone to mow your

yard in the first place," I pointed out. "And besides that, you're going to be out a hundred bucks when I leave."

Mart smiled and shook his head as he put his smoke out in the ashtray.

"That hundred's been riding around in my wallet for better than 20 years, boy; it's nothing more to me than a scrap of paper. Giving it to you just makes more sense than taking it to the grave with me.

"As far as me not hiring someone to mow the lawn; you're probably right. I doubt I would have gone out of my way to hunt up someone willing to take it on but that's not to say I didn't want it done. As hard as this might be for you to believe, there aren't that many people in this world willing to put in an honest day's work for a day's pay. I like the idea of having the place tidied up; I feel bad about not keeping it up in the first place but I just haven't had the gumption to do much of anything since Mary passed. Make no mistake about it, though; if someone had come knocking for the job I'd have hired them on the spot."

Mart paused to give me an opening but I didn't say anything. Truth be told, I honestly didn't believe the old man gave a tin shit what kind of shape his yard was in but, since there was no way for me to be sure, I decided I probably owed him the benefit of the doubt.

"Now I'm going to pick you up a few things in town today," Mart continued. "As far as I'm concerned you don't owe me a thing but if you've really got a problem with that you can pay me back after I pay you for your work. Now how 'bout it?"

'Oh, man, would my dad love to meet you,' I thought to myself. But even as the thought formed I remembered the way Mart tore into me after I lied to him about my name and age and I suddenly knew Leo Malone wouldn't have gotten anything more than the time of day from this old man...and maybe not even that. The only thing my dad had a real talent for, his real forte in life that he could have used to be a success had he never taken that first drink, was an uncanny ability to know which buttons to push to convince a complete stranger that he had just met a kindred spirit; an 'if-but-for-the-grace-of-God-go-I' kind of guy who had made a poor choice or two but had learned his lesson- learned it well- and was now back on the right track... except he had to ask (and he felt horrible about having to do it since it was his own fault for being in this situation in the first place) for this one little favor. I'd say my dad was able to work roughly ninety-five percent of the people he set his sights on but the only shtick that ever would have worked on this old man was straight ahead honesty; the one technique my dad had never been able to get a handle on.

It suddenly occurred to me that maybe I wasn't the smartest person in the room. Like Mart said, he had a lifetime of experience over me and it was obvious he was nobody's fool. If he thought paying me for my work was the right thing to do, who was I to argue?

"I guess that'll be okay," I finally agreed. "But I don't want you spending a lot of money on me."

"Tell you what," Mart said, butting his cigarette out in the ashtray, "why don't you take the afternoon off and ride along with me to see for yourself. It's too damn hot for you to be working out there in the sun anyway."

I thought it over for a second. What was the rush in getting the yard done?

"Okay," I said.

"All right then," Mart slapped his hands on his thighs and stood up. "Grab yourself another can of pop why don't you and we'll head on out."

The ride into Greenville was nice. Mart was a slow driver, one who seemed to prefer dirt roads to tar, but I didn't mind. Poking along down gravel country lanes with the windows open and the truck's a.m. radio playing country/western oldies sure beat the hell out of the white knuckle car joisting I was used to when I rode anywhere with my dad. Mesmerized by the countryside slipping by, I dropped my arm outside to ride the truck's slipstream with the palm of my hand as I stared out my window. The buzzing siren sound of emerging cicadas pierced the road rumblings of the pickup with the regularity of evenly placed fence posts and the air was flavored with the smell of green growing plants and sun-baked dust. I had a sudden, minor epiphany as I realized I felt, at least for the moment, content.

"Why are we going to Greenville?" I asked just to make conversation. "Trufant's a lot closer to your house, isn't it?"

"Oh, we'll be swinging by there on the way home," Mart answered, "but Trufant doesn't have a clothing store any more... not since they opened up this new Thrifty Acres store over in Greenville. Won't be long before that damn place runs Lemire's and DeWall's into the ground too, I guess, and then Trufant won't even be a town any more."

Clothes? The old man wanted to buy me some clothes? I was excited and worried at the same time. I'd kill for a new pair of Levi's- I'd never owned a new pair of blue jeans in my life- but clothes were expensive.

“Now take it easy, son,” Mart said, glancing over at me. “Those duds you’re wearing there are about worn clean through and you know it. We’re going to pick you up some blue jeans, a couple t-shirts, and either some pajamas or some underpants; I don’t care which.” The old man shifted in his seat and scowled. “ I’ve got to tell you, boy, I’m not too keen on the idea of you spending any more nights out on my couch in your birthday suit.”

While I was kind of embarrassed at having the old man mentioning my lack of underwear (a supply of socks and underwear usually made up the bulk of my Christmas presents every year but the previous Christmas had been pretty much a bust, what with mom dying and all), hearing Mart say the word ‘underpants’ tickled me for some reason. It just wasn’t a word you would ever expect an old man to say.

“Okay,” I said. At a quarter an hour I knew it would probably take at least a couple of weeks to earn enough money to reimburse Mart for the things he was talking about buying.... and that didn’t sound all bad.

Mart threw a surprised glance at me before looking back to the road. Evidently he’d been expecting an argument.

“You know,” he said, glancing back over at me with a raised eyebrow and a hopeful look, “Greenville does have a barbershop or two; you must be itching to get that mop of yours lopped off, aren’t you?”

“No sir,” I quickly shook my head. I liked my hair the way it was...kind of thought it made me look like David Cassidy, if you want to know the truth.

Obviously bewildered, Mart shook his head and frowned his disapproval.

“All right,” he sighed under his breath. “But don’t go blaming me if the salesclerk tries to sell you a dress.”

I smiled and turned back to look out my window.

I was content.

Mart ended up spending nineteen dollars and eighty-two cents on the clothes I picked out that day, eighteen cents short of my self imposed limit of twenty-dollars, and I walked out of the store carrying a plain brown grocery bag filled with two pairs of bell bottom blue jeans, three brown colored t-shirts, three pairs of socks, and a three pack of Fruit of the Loom underwear. Carrying the bag was sweet agony; I had desperately wanted to wear the clothes out of the store but I was too self-conscious about possibly looking like a dork to ask if I could. Of all the ages to be, fourteen has got to be about the worst, you're old enough to know you're not quite a kid anymore but too young to not want to act like one.

Climbing back into the truck, we drove on over to Trufant for the groceries. I tried to get Mart to lock the truck before we went into the Food Mart but he just laughed and shook his head. He didn't even take the keys out of the ignition!

"Tell you what, boy," he said mildly, walking around the front of the truck. "If those clothes aren't sitting on that seat when we get through in here, I'll eat that truck for supper tonight. Now come on."

I took what I figured was going to be my last look at my shopping bag of crisp, dye smelling new clothes, locked and closed my door, and followed Mart into the store.

Both the truck and my clothes were still there when we came back out, but since my door was locked, I couldn't get into the truck. Mart had both a cigarette and the truck's engine going before he noticed me waiting outside my door. Shaking his head, he leaned over and unlocked my door. I climbed in and we took off.

Mart glanced over at me as we rolled past the Trufant City

Limits sign (pop. 141) on our way out of town.

"You in any rush to get back, boy?" he asked.

"I guess not," I shrugged, casting a forlorn eye on my bag of new clothes. "Why?"

Letting off the gas, Mart downshifted and steered the truck off the blacktop onto another gravel road.

"Thought I might as well give you the fifty cent tour," he said, working the column shifter. "Show you the sights."

Most of the 'sights' Mart showed me that day were just that; empty, overgrown sights where some house, store, or sawmill had once stood years or even decades earlier. Sometimes we'd get out of the truck and Mart would point out where a dam use to be before it crumbled and washed out back in 1926 or where an old church had stood before it burned to the ground in 1937, but most of the time we'd just stop on whatever road or two track we happened to be on and Mart would tell me what use to be there.

The last place we stopped that day, a roofless, tumbled down log cabin hidden behind a huge stand of lilacs, was just a half a mile or so up the road from Mart's house. I had walked past it twice the night before and never noticed it. Easing the old truck through the ditch, Mart drove around the lilacs and stopped facing the sidewall of the cabin.

"This use to be the cook shack for one of the logging gangs that worked this area just after the Civil War," Mart said, turning off the engine. "My folks started out here in this cabin after daddy bought the land from the Converse Lumber Company back in 1879. Their plan was to live here for a year or two until daddy could get around to building a stick built house but then one thing led to another and they ended up living here for nearly eleven years."

Staring at the cabin, Mart slipped a cigarette into his mouth before opening his door and climbing down out of the truck. Rolling my eyes a little (all I wanted to do was get back to the house so I could take a shower and try on those new clothes) I sighed as I pushed my door open to get out. Leading the way, the old man threaded his way through the underbrush around to the other side of the cabin. I caught up to him as he paused a few feet from the building to light his smoke.

"This here's the only door," he said, nodding toward the gap tooth hole in the wall we were facing, "and there aren't any windows; I can't even begin to imagine what it must have been like to live in there over an entire winter. My folks use to tell us kids stories about how they could go from November to April without ever seeing another soul. The roof's gone now, of course, but it was still there when I use to hike out here as a boy and I'm here to tell you that walking into that cabin was just about like walking into a cave. The door faces to the North, you see, so it never mattered where the sun happened to be in the sky; if you were more than a foot or two away from the doorway you couldn't see squat. They tell me the lumber companies use to build them that way so as to keep the loggers from getting a good look at the food the cook was feeding them and I don't doubt that for a minute."

The old man paused and gave me a conspiratorial little smile.

"Back when I was just a little shaver my daddy use to tell me the only reason I had so many older brothers and sisters and no younger ones was because the family had finally moved from here into a real house with windows and ma could finally see to run away from him when he wanted some loving. 'Why, you wouldn't be here today if it weren't for your ma stubbing her toe on that footstool,' daddy would say, pointing at the footstool or chair or whatever piece of furniture that happened to be closest whenever he was telling me this. I was too young at the time to get the joke but it sure use to embarrass the hell out of ma, or at least she'd act like it did anyway. She'd take a little swat at him if he were close enough or give him the old evil eye if he wasn't, but you could see she was just doing it for show."

The old man trailed off, his smile fading as he stood there looking at the cabin.

"There was a time when this was about my favorite place in the world," he said solemnly.

Taking that statement to mean Mart was about ready to head back, I watched and waited for him to start for the truck but he didn't make any bones about leaving. Shifting my weight from one foot to the other I started passing the time by picturing how cool I would look in my new jeans when (if, I amended silently with another eye roll) we got back to the house.

"Remember me telling you how the sight of all those books in your suitcase reminded me of a friend I once had?" Mart asked. The note of quiet pleasure that had been in his voice most of the afternoon was gone.

"Sure," I answered. The old man had my full attention now. "David, right?"

"That's right," he nodded. Noticing an old uprooted pine tree lying nearby, he walked over and sat down.

"Have a seat, boy," he said, patting the barkless trunk. "This might take a minute or two."

"His full name was David Joseph Johansson," Mart said after I sat down, "and this is where he lived.

"His family moved up here from Ohio after they lost their house and everything else they owned in a fire. They happened to move into this particular cabin because Ester's brother, Lars Christianson, the owner of the general uptown, was looking to help his sister somehow and he knew this place was just standing out here empty. Now Lars didn't think much of Ester's choice of a husband- Leonard Johansson had a good 30 years on Ester and was nothing more than a cradle robber according to Lars- but he did love his sister and he offered my daddy the opportunity to tear up a forty-nine dollar credit note Lars was holding at the store in exchange for a year's lease on this cabin. Daddy took him up on it and that was that."

Dropping his cigarette to the ground and toeing it out, Mart looked over and gave me a knowing little look.

"Now I know this must sound like ancient history to you, son," he said, "but the day will come soon enough where you'll understand what I mean when I tell you it really wasn't that long ago, at least not to me. Someday, and it'll be here so fast it'll make your head spin, you'll be the one talking with your son or daughter about this ancient year of 1974 and you'll remember sitting here on this old felled pine listening to me... and then you'll know."

I remembered the time warp sensation I had felt when I first saw Cindy step out of Charley's Bar (could it have been just two nights ago?) and slowly nodded my head. I understood what he was trying to tell me... or at least I thought I did. Probably one of the best things about being a kid is the serene inability to understand how short your time on this earth really is.

Out on the road a black, older style Camaro screamed by like a low flying jet, its dual straight pipes strafing the trees with high-test exhaust. Looking pained, Mart waited for the noise to fade before speaking again.

"It seemed like David and I were friends even before we met," he said, remembering. "We talked about it later and we both agreed that it was like we had always known each other, like we had been best friends in a past life somehow. It felt almost magical at the time and now that I've lived twelve years beyond my allotted three score and ten, I know that it was. I've never had a friend since that meant as much to me as David did and I only knew him for a little over a year.

"We met for the first time- this was a day or two after his family moved here so I'm guessing it was late March or early April of ot' four- down on Tank Creek. I happened to be there that day just because I loved to fish and Tank

Creek was the only water I could get to that spring that wasn't still ringed in ice. David was fishing there because his family didn't have anything to eat for supper that night. He didn't come right out and tell me that, of course, David always kept his family's troubles to himself, at least at first, but the fact that he was using sewing thread straight off the bobbin and a bent straight pin to fish with clued me in. We didn't talk much that afternoon but when it came time for me to start thinking about headin' for home I skinned the six brookies I'd landed and added them to the two little chubs David had somehow managed to catch. He didn't want to take them at first but I managed to talk him into it and then we made plans to walk to school together the next day. Just like that," Mart snapped his fingers, "we were friends. We came to know each other as well as we knew ourselves that spring and we talked about everything; we pondered life and death and bugs and girls and anything else that occurred to us. David helped me with my schoolwork while we were in school and I showed him how to hunt and trap and fish when we weren't. He told me about living in a city and I told him stories about my family." Mart stared over at a specific spot a few feet away from the cabin wall.

"And later," he said, "after I saw Leonard Johansson break his own arm with an ax, David told me about his daddy."

"Wait," I interrupted. I thought I must have heard that wrong. "You saw some guy break his own arm? On purpose?"

"Yep," Mart nodded. "It happened on the morning of the last day of school before summer vacation. David and I always walked to school together and I was waiting for him over there," the old man turned on the log and pointed to a spot a hundred feet away, "where the road used to run before the county straightened it. I'd been waiting there a while, gotten bored, and had climbed up into the lower branches of a lightning scarred oak. My plan when I climbed up there was to drop down and scare the daylights out of either David, who usually came out first, or, if they managed to beat him out the door somehow, his three sisters, who always walked together. I don't know how long I was up there but it started getting to be kind of late and the last day of school was one day I certainly didn't want to have to stay after and wash blackboards. I'd just about decided to climb down and beat it for school by myself when I heard the cabin door open. Knowing it had to be either David or his sisters, I hunkered down behind a leafy part of the branch where I could see whoever came out without them seeing me and waited.

"David was the first to come walking out of the cabin and I saw right away that something wasn't right; he was still wearing the ragged old bedshirt he slept in and he was walking like a kid that had a whippin' coming... a razor strap type of whippin'. I saw him eye the base of the tree I was hiding in when he came out, looking to see if I was standing there waiting for him like I usually did before school, but since I was up in the tree rather than milling around beside it, he didn't see me. I couldn't tell whether he was disappointed or relieved when he saw that I wasn't there, his expression never changed. His sisters came walking out right behind him and they all looked to be in the same boat as their brother. They weren't dressed for school either and all three of them looked worried and scared half to death. Helen, the youngest at six or seven years old, was crying some and holding David's hand, trailing along blindly behind him with her head down and the index finger of her free hand poked in her mouth. The sun was just breaking over the tree line beyond and the dew mist rising up from the ground swirled around them as they walked across the yard to an ancient old cant bench left over from days of the loggers. Helen tried to climb into David's lap when they all sat down but he wouldn't let her. He sat her down next to him and her thumb replaced the finger in her mouth as she looked at the ground below her feet.

"David's ma was already out of the cabin when I looked back that way. She was wearing the gingham dress she always wore when she was expected to work in her brother's store uptown, but her feet were bare and she was carrying a long, thin, candy box-looking thing, holding it to her chest with both arms and she had a gray goose feather sticking up out of her right fist. She stepped away from the cabin slow, kinda glancing back at her heels without moving her head much. I couldn't see anything or anyone lurking in the cabin behind her but as soon as she figured she was in the clear she hurried over to her babies and said some things to them. I couldn't hear what she was saying as she was talking low and I was too far away, but there wasn't anything wrong with my eyes; even from a hundred feet away I could see she looked as lost and scared as her children, maybe worse, and that's when I started getting anxious. While it had been bad seeing David and his sisters all looking like they were about to meet their maker, they were just kids like me. Kids always look scared when they get into trouble. I was figuring maybe David and his sisters had gotten to arguing and fighting or something that morning and they'd all been sent out here to wait for a good tongue lashing from one of their folks, but to see that same helpless look of despair in their ma's eyes, well, that just made my blood run cold. Something bad was happening here, I could feel it radiating off the five of them all the way across the yard; something unnatural and secret and I knew I didn't want to know anything more about it than what I'd already seen. I didn't care who saw me doing 'er , I was climbing down out of that tree and running for home. And that's when David's daddy stepped outside."

Mart paused, his arms locked with his hands on his knees, staring at the empty doorway a few feet away. I was fascinated with the story and impatient for him to go on, any remaining thought of my new clothes completely forgotten.

"What happened?" I prodded after waiting for what seemed like an appropriate amount of time.

Mart blinked a couple times and sat back on the log. Heaving a sigh, he pulled out a cigarette and his Zippo. I noticed his hand shaking a little as he held the lighter to his Chesterfield.

"I didn't know it then," he said, glancing at me as he slipped the lighter back into his pocket, "but Leonard Johansson was losing his mind. He wasn't completely round the bend yet- though I expect David and his sisters may have begged to differ- but he was better than half way into the curve. He didn't look crazy, at least not in public; to most folks he never would look like anything more than a harmless, rail thin old man, right up to the day the county sheriff carted him off to the psychiatric hospital over to Traverse City. And, since Leonard had never learned to speak any more than a simple word or two of English since he stepped off the boat, most folks in town wouldn't even have noticed had he come right out and told them he believed he was the second coming of Christ. Of course Trufant still had a sizable Danish community back then, and while the Danes were normally a closed mouthed bunch when it came to one of their own, somebody would have said something to someone had Leonard talked out of turn to any of them, and that hadn't happened. As far as I knew, David's daddy was just as sane as mine, and that made everything that went on that morning all the worse."

"Leonard took one step out of the cabin and stopped. He stood there just outside the doorway looking tense and on edge and standing ramrod straight. He was wearing a black wool suit- it must have been a horrible smelling thing as I was going to catch a whiff or two of it all the way across the yard before that morning was over- and he was cradling a Bible high on his chest," Mart brought his arm up to his breast to demonstrate without looking away from the cabin doorway. "His eyes were wide open and glassy and even from as far away as I was I could see they had this wild animal look to them. He stood there and looked around, his bald head jerking a few degrees at a time like he was searching the woods for something. He looked down his nose as he searched, his chin up and mouth open with his tongue sticking out a little ways, wiggling around every couple seconds like he could taste things in the air. His skin was winter pale and sickly looking, his arms and legs little more than sticks inside his smelly suit. I had a bad moment when he looked over in my direction- I knew he was staring right into my eyes when he looked to the tree I was hiding in and I came damn close to shimming down and making a run for it- but then his head swiveled another few degrees and I knew he'd missed seeing me. Looking over to the bench I saw the kids were all still staring at the ground. Ester, who was watching Leonard, looked scared to death. She had that candy-box looking thing she'd been carrying setting on her lap, the goose feather poised at the ready in her right hand over the strings of what I could now see was a harpsichord. Leonard barked something in Danish right about then and she started strumming a song I recognized; Bringing in the Sheaves, it was. Ester and the kids all started singing, only it was screwy and backwards sounding to me since they were singing in Dutch. Leonard stood right there where he was, looking down his nose at them as they sang, his tongue slipping in and out of his mouth and clutching his Bible tightly to his chest. He mostly stood perfectly still- except for the snaky thing he was doing with his tongue- but every once and a while his whole body would seem to twitch, to vibrate, almost, and even though the temperature was a bit on the chilly side, I could see the top of his head was shiny with sweat. The sight of him reminded me of a wagon load of nitroglycerin, ready to go off at the first bump in the road."

Looking down, Mart shook his head as he took the last drag from his smoke and dropped the butt to the ground.

"You ever heard a harpsichord being played, boy?" he asked.

"No sir," I answered.

"Well, it ain't an instrument to get a man's toe tapping, let me tell you," he said, smiling a little in spite of himself. "It's a slow, cumbersome sounding thing that's killed many a good church sing-a-long... and the folks at a sing-a-long are there because they want to sing! Ester and her kids weren't in any more of a mood to sing than I was, hiding up in that tree, and it showed. They weren't but about halfway through the second verse when Leonard started slapping his hand on his thigh and bobbing his head up and down to get them to speed things up a bit. Now since Ester wasn't any great shakes at being a harpsichord player in the first place, having Leonard pushing her that way made her all the more nervous and fumble-fingered. She started missing notes, the kids lost track of the words and little Helen started crying again. And that's when Leonard went off. He screamed a word in Dutch, 'Enough' or 'Stop' or something along those lines it must have been, screamed it at the top of his lungs, and everything got real quiet.

"Now Leonard Johansson's scream alone had been more than enough to scare the living hell right out of me, I never heard another man nor woman scream that way before or since, but it was the sound of the absolute silence in the woods *after* he screamed that really got my skin crawling. I knew the woods, you see, I knew you could startle things quiet by making a loud noise- shooting a gun, for instance, or yelling- but the thing is, the things you startle don't <u>stay</u> quiet, not for very long; crickets never stop chirpin' for more than five or ten seconds, frogs, maybe a little longer than that, and birds a little longer still, but not this time. This time it felt like every living, calling thing within earshot of the old man's voice had been struck dead in its tracks or on the wing. The only thing I could hear was the sound of my own heart slamming away in my chest and that sounded so loud to me I was honestly afraid Leonard might hear it, hundred feet away or not, and thinking about <u>that</u> only made my heart beat even harder and louder until it was beating so hard it was actually vibrating the branch I was stretched out on. I could see the leaves around me shaking in time with the pounding I was hearing in my ears. I was afraid to move a muscle; it was all I could do to just keep breathing while I watched and waited to see what Leonard was going to do. And that's when Leonard saw the crow."

I felt like I'd just taken a drink out of a pop can and come away with a mouthful of milk. A crow!? What in the world could a crow have to do with this?

"David told me later it was the worst thing that could have happened that day, having his daddy see that crow perched up there like that," Mart went on. "You see David's daddy hadn't always acted as peculiar as he was acting that morning. No, from what David told me, old Leonard had once been a fairly normal man, right up until about a year before the fire that sent his family packing from Ohio. And it was Leonard that set that fire, too, by the way, but that's neither here nor there for right now.

"David said the first time he noticed that his daddy's wheels might be a bit wobbly was when the old man suddenly developed an unnatural fear of crows and ravens... said they weren't birds at all but Watchers sent by Satan. David said he asked his daddy once why he called them that but his daddy didn't answer him; he just stared at David all squinty eyed and suspicious looking, like maybe he was wondering if David might not be a Watcher sent by Satan too. David told me it wasn't but a month or two after that that Leonard started talking to a wooden figure of Saint Christopher that David's ma had in the house... and it wasn't too long after that that Leonard started hearing that piece of wood talking back to him! David said his daddy'd take that carving of Saint Christopher down from the fireplace mantle, set it up on the table where he could look the old boy right in the eye and the two of them would have regular conversations together! And then there were other things he started doing, too; he quit bathing regular, he wouldn't go outside during the day unless it were cloudy, he took to waking up his wife and children in the middle of the night every couple of weeks to preach at them for hours on end about how Satan and minions were everywhere (according to what Leonard told his family, he and he alone could see the demons that constantly surrounded them and because he could do that, Satan was likely to one day come after his soul through one of them), and then, after he and his family moved up here, Leonard started having night terrors." Mart paused, looking at the cabin. "Can you imagine what that must have been like in there?" he asked without looking at me, shaking his head. "Waking up to the sound of your daddy screaming like he's being skinned alive and not being able to see a damn thing? My God, it's a wonder the whole bunch wasn't a little loopy."

I could imagine what that was like and I agreed with Mart; it was a wonder the whole family wasn't a little loopy.

I'd had night terrors for a while as a little kid. Two or three times a year I'd wake up ('come to' would probably be a more accurate term) to find myself sitting up in bed, shrieking. I'd usually been screaming for quite a while before I woke up; the lights in my room would already be on and my folks would be there, dad in his boxers and mom in a nighty without her robe, both looking helpless and scared. A couple of times I was sitting on the edge of my bed when I woke up, my dad frantically rubbing my legs with Old Spice after shave because I'd been screaming something about broken bones while massaging my legs with my hands, but most times I wasn't screaming about anything that could be understood. Other than being a little hoarse the next day, these episodes never really bothered me that much but mom, dad, and Cindy always looked worn out and shell-shocked the next morning.

"Well anyway," Mart said, getting back on track. "Leonard spied this crow sitting up in a tree and the sight of it just seemed to knock all the starch right out of his backbone; his whole body just sort of... sort of sagged, I don't know any better way to put it. I hadn't seen the crow yet, though it wouldn't have made a lick of difference if I had; a crow was just another bird to me, so I thought maybe the old boy was having some kinda spell or something, but then I saw he was staring at a particular spot about midway between the two of us and a little off to my right. I looked around over in the direction he was staring and saw this big black crow perched on a lower limb of a dead poplar. I guess it might sound kind of crazy now, but from where I was over in that tree, it looked like that crow was staring right back at Leonard... kinda watching him, I guess you could say. I didn't understand it then and I don't understand it now. If you've ever looked at a crow for more than a second or two you know they never stand still or stare at one thing for any amount of time, not unless they're dead or sleeping that is, but this one was doing just that. He stood there just as still as a rock on flat ground, watching Leonard with his shiny black eyes. It wasn't right... none of it was. I remember I'd just started to wonder if maybe I weren't still home in bed having a bad dream when all of a sudden that damned crow cawed the loudest, nastiest caw I'd ever heard in my life and that's when Leonard went stark ravin' mad.

"He started off by throwing his Bible at the crow, but he threw it wrong; the pages of the thing opened up the second it left his hand and it came fluttering down not ten foot from where he stood. The crow just sat there on that dead branch and watched. Leonard started tearing at his clothes, his hair, his mouth. He started screaming 'NEE! NEE! NEE!' over and over and over. He ripped an arm loose from his suit coat. His lips were bleeding. He charged toward the crow, running a couple steps before stopping and stomping his foot and then running back. He grabbed up a handful of sod and threw that, screaming in pain this time even before the dirt left his hand as his right arm tore free of its socket with a loud, wet sounding 'pop' that I heard all the way across the yard. Switching to his left arm, he grabbed up a dead stick and tried to throw that but missed by a mile. His eyes bugged as he searched the ground around him for something else to throw, his right arm dangling at his side like a length of cordwood swinging from a nail. He found a pebble and threw that but it was too light to go even as far as his Bible had gone. Seeing there wasn't anything else handy to throw, he turned on his heel and ran back into the cabin. I looked back at the crow and just caught a glimpse of him flying away into the woods; he must have taken flight the very instant Leonard had turned his back to go into the cabin. Everything was quiet for about a half second and then Leonard came roaring back out, swinging a two-bitted ax with his one good arm and screaming something that sounded like 'NEE KRAAI!' as he wound up to give the ax a heave. He never looked to see if the crow was still there.

"Leonard threw that ax with everything he had and then ended up on the ground in a heap, hurting his arm again in the process by the sound of it. The ax never even came close to the tree the crow had been in; it went whistling end for end on an arched path right toward the bench where David and his ma and sisters were sitting. They'd been watching all this, of course, and they were all able to scramble clear before the ax came down but the damn thing ended up landing short of the bench. It hit a root, took a bad bounce and shot off toward Helen. I saw David reach out to pull her out of the way but it was too late; the ax hit her on the head and she dropped like a bag of rocks. It all happened so fast I wasn't too sure she didn't have that ax head buried right between the eyes...and since Leonard was watching from where he'd landed in the dirt after throwing the ax, he couldn't have seen exactly what had happened either and I figured he was probably thinking the same thing, that Helen might be dead... but he sure didn't act like it."

"Why?" I asked. "What'd he do?"

"Well, he looked to see if the crow was gone, that was the first thing. Then, after seeing that it was, he crawled over to where his Bible lay spread out in the dirt, straightened it out with his one good hand and started leafing through the pages, first one way then the other, until he found a passage he was looking for. Then he just started reading. He never looked up or even asked if his girl were alive or dead, he just sat there on his knees in the dirt reading to himself.

"Helen got up a couple minutes later while Leonard was still reading. She'd end up sportin' a handsome set of shiners for a week or two after that morning but considering what could have happened had that ax spun another half turn, she got off pretty light. Ester tried to tell her husband that Helen was all right, she even picked the little girl up and carried her over to show the old man, but Leonard never looked up, he just kept on reading. She finally gave up and carried Helen back to the bench where they both sat back down with David and the other two girls and we all waited while Leonard knelt there in the dirt, reading his Bible. I don't know about those on the bench but I for one spent that time watching for crows. None showed up but the day went on to get worse anyway.

"It felt longer at the time but I'm guessing Leonard didn't sit there for more five or ten minutes before he finally closed his bible and pushed himself up to his feet. He was a might unsteady at first, which wasn't at all surprising considering his age and the way he'd been tearing around, but he eventually got his sea legs under him and he made his way over to Ester and the children. He said something to them in Dutch and everybody stood up and filed over to one side of the bench. I noticed all five of them were holding hands.

"Leonard recited aloud a single verse from the Bible. I couldn't understand what he was saying, of course, but David told me later it was a verse from the book of Mark, chapter nine, verse forty-three." Mart closed his eyes and recited:

"And if thy hand offend thee, cut it off; for it is better for thee to enter into life maimed than, having two hands, to go into hell, into the fire that never shall be quenched."

Mart opened his eyes and looked at me. "That's the verse Leonard recited to his family," he said, "and as soon as he finished, he reached down and picked up the ax."

"Oh man," I moaned. "Is that really in the Bible?"

"It is," Mart nodded. "I was the lucky one that day because I couldn't understand Dutch and I didn't have any idea what was coming, but Ester and David and the girls, they had to have known what Leonard was going to do from the first sentence of that verse and there wasn't a damn thing they could do to stop it. Whether because he'd thrown his Bible or because he'd thrown the ax that hurt his daughter, I'll never know, but Leonard's hand had offended him and he was aiming to chop it off."

"But you said you seen him break his arm, not cut his hand off," I said.

"I did and that's exactly what happened," Mart answered. "Once Leonard finished that verse he didn't waste any time; he got down on his knees in front of the bench, grabbed his right arm up with his left hand and laid it down along the center of the seat, picked up the ax and let 'er fly. He did all this in one motion, bam, bam, bam, and I think that's probably why he missed his mark with the blade; he grabbed too low on the handle and his swing went long. The ax head came down on the far side of the cant, missing it completely, and that allowed the handle to come smashing down on his scrawny old arm just above the wrist...it sounded like a dropped hardboiled egg hitting the floor and Leonard just keeled right over on his side. Everything was perfectly still for a second and then all hell broke loose. Ester fainted dead away, David threw up, the girls started screaming and crying and carrying on, and I took off. I dropped down out of that tree and headed for the hills without ever looking back." Mart pursed his lips as he leaned forward and rested his elbows on his knees. He stared down at his hands.

"I've always felt guilty about running away like that, leaving David alone to deal with that mess in his yard," he said. "I try telling myself I was only twelve and there really wasn't anything I could have done even if I had stayed, but that never seems to cut any ice with my conscience. I was old enough to know I had a choice between running away or staying and helping my friend and I chose to run." Mart lapsed into silence for a minute before pulling out his handkerchief and blowing his nose.

"David saw me running away that day, you see," he said, glancing at me as he tucked his handkerchief back into his pocket. "He said he didn't hold it against me, said he'd have done the same had he been in my shoes, but I could see I'd hurt him and I felt bad because of it. I promised myself I'd make it up to him someday but he ran away that following spring and I never got the chance.

"David had mentioned running away from home a couple of times before he actually went and did it but I'd never really took him to be serious about it. Not that I blamed him for doing it, you understand- his daddy had taken to living in the outhouse as soon as it turned warm enough that year- but I never thought he'd ever leave his sisters behind and I never in a million years thought he'd ever leave without telling me goodbye. Turned out I was wrong. He ran away in May of 1905 and I never heard from him again."

"What about his mom and his sisters?" I asked. "Did he ever get in touch with them?"

"Don't know," Mart shrugged. "Ester and the girls packed up and moved back down to Ohio a while later after Leonard ended up getting himself committed to the loony bin upstate for popping one of his eyes out with a sewing awl. Ester's brother, Lars, had died of consumption just a month or two earlier and with him gone there really wasn't any reason for them to stay. They left and never came back."

"Man," I said, shaking my head. Compared to this David kid, I really didn't have much to bitch about. My dad might not have had a lot going for him but at least he wasn't crazy.

"Well, boy," Mart said, standing up. "We've got some things out in the truck that'll turn if we don't get em home and into the fridge." I pushed myself up and we started back around to the other side of the cabin.

"Why did the books in my suitcase remind you of David?" I asked as we walked up to the truck. "Did he like to read a lot?"

"Oh, that boy lived to read," Mart answered in mock disgust. "Used to drive me nuts the way he always had to have his nose buried in a book... and a lot of times it'd be a book he had already read before! He didn't own any books himself, but his Uncle Lars had a whole slew of 'em and he used to let David borrow one book a week. Getting that kid to do anything for the first day or two after he'd picked up a new book was like pulling teeth. Why, half the times we went fishing he wouldn't even bring a pole along- he'd just bring a book and read! The first thing I thought of when I figured out you'd most likely come from California carrying nothing but a suitcase full of books was to remember David sitting down to the lake with a book instead of a fishing pole. And then I remembered everything else."

Reaching the truck, we opened the doors and climbed in. Mart closed his door and settled back in the seat with one hand draped over the steering wheel, looking out the windshield at the back of the cabin

"I spent a lot of time wondering what had become of David when I was younger," he said. "And then, after Mary and I started having kids of our own, I spent a lot of time trying to forget about him."

"Why?" I asked, surprised. "Why'd you want to forget about him?"

Mart stared out the window and thought for a minute.

"Because I ran away when he needed me," he said quietly. "I'd always regretted it, of course, but after I became a father I couldn't think of David anymore without wondering what a difference it might have made in his life had he seen his best friend running to help him rather than running away."

Mart turned and gave me a measured look.

"You remember the last thing you said to me before you walked out the door last night?"

'I don't know if you made that promise to God or not...'

It was my turn to look down at my hands; I remembered all right.

"Well, I wasn't lying to you when I told you I had promised God I'd help any kid he sent my way but I wasn't exactly telling you the whole truth, either.

"I was twenty-three years old and the father of two when I made that promise. David had long passed the age of needing the kind of help I was asking of God by then, but I had to do something to make up for running out on him the one time he truly needed me. The only thing I could think to do was to ask God for his help. I couldn't go back in time and undo what I had done, but who's to say God couldn't go back and watch over my friend somehow? God can do anything, right? All I had to offer him in return was my word that I'd do the same but I guess God must have known I was good for it because the guilt I'd been living with just went away.

"I went on to think of David once and a while after God and I reached our agreement but it wasn't like before. I still regretted what I had done but I didn't cringe inside the second I thought of him anymore, I was finally able to accept the choice I'd made as a twelve-year-old boy. I'd wonder about him, picture him happy, maybe with a wife and some kids of his own somewhere, and I'd remember the magical feeling of the time we had before he left. Then I'd look up and give God a little nod to let him know I was still good for my end of the bargain. After a while I thought of David less and less until finally I guess I just forgot about him and my promise altogether, but God never forgot. He remembered and he sent you."

I looked at the old man in wonder. 'Why couldn't you have been my father?' I thought.

"Well, I guess that's it for the tour," Mart said, sitting up straight and pushing in the clutch. Lighting a cigarette with one hand, he reached down and keyed the truck into life with the other. "I'll bet you're just chomping at the bit to slip into your new duds, huh boy?" he asked, checking his mirror as he shifted the truck into reverse.

"I'm sorry," I said. Mart stopped and gave me a puzzled look.

"I thought you were lying to me last night when you told me that stuff about promising God you'd help a kid some day," I said. "It was just too weird... too convenient, you know? I thought you were lying just so I'd tell you things about myself so I left. I didn't know what kind of person you were then, but now I think I do... and I'm sorry."

Mart smiled.

"Too convenient, eh?" he said, scratching his chin. "Well, like our mothers always said, boy, 'God works in mysterious ways'."

I smiled back and shook my head. I wasn't so sure I was ready to buy into Mart's God thing yet, but that was okay. Now that I knew he honestly believed in what he'd been telling me, I could at least begin to consider the possibility.

"Let's go home, son," Mart said. Letting off on the clutch, he turned and backed out onto the road.

Looking out my window, I could feel the excitement growing in my heart as the last two things Mart had said cycled through my head.

Let's go home, son. God works in mysterious ways.

Let's go home...

Maybe I could believe.

I found a couple of odd things hidden in the weeds the next morning. Mart wasn't around; he'd already been up and tinkering with the lawn mower by the time I emerged from the house that morning (I was never one to sleep in but I'd slept like the dead that night and didn't wake up until after nine!) and was just climbing into his truck when I came out. Before backing down the driveway he told me he was going into town for some fresh lawn mower gas and then he was going to stop by the cemetery for a spell on the way back. I didn't have any idea how long an average 'spell' was but I figured he'd probably be gone an hour or so.

I was swinging the scythe over in the furthest corner of the yard from the house when the blade slammed into something that was a whole lot more solid than weeds I was used to.

"OW... DAMN!" I yelled.

I let go of the handle and spun around, shaking my hands in a futile attempt to ease the shocktingle that was stinging my blistered palms. As the pain slowly faded I turned back to see what I had hit and saw the scythe was suspended in midair right where I had left it. Thinking I had stuck it in a rotted tree stump or something, I pushed the weeds around the scythe down with my foot and saw I had buried the blade into the side of a thick and partially rotted board that was sticking straight up out of the ground. Curious, I pried the scythe free, made short work of the weeds that surrounded the piece of wood and got down on my knees to check it out.

The portion of the board sticking out of the ground was at least a couple inches thick, a foot or so wide, and about a foot and a half tall. It had obviously been painted white at one time but most of the paint was long gone; all that remained were a few cracked flakes that disappeared into dust when I touched them. Resting my hand on the top of the board I gave it a little jiggle to see how sturdy it was and jumped as it let out an immediate crack. While it didn't break, I knew it would have snapped off clean had I hit it broadside with the scythe rather than on its edge. Being a city boy, I figured the board had been planted there to mark an old garden border or something and was just about to get back to work when I peeked over the top and saw deeply carved letters and numbers on the other side. Shuffling around on my knees to get a better look, I sat back on my heels and read:

MINDY
1958-1969
SHE WAS A
GOOD DOG

All told I found seven grave markers in that corner of the yard; a tiny, two row cemetery with four graves in the back at the extreme edge of the yard and three more a few feet in front of them, closer to the house. Six of them (including the first one I found) were simple planks of wood, each one in progressively worse shape than the one before it. While I could still read the names and dates on the other two markers in the front row (Sammy 1941-1954 and Rex 1935-1939) the remaining three planks in the back row were little more than dried pieces of driftwood.

The seventh and last marker was really something special. Although it was obvious from the dates inscribed in it that this grave was older than the rest, the marker itself was an actual granite tombstone complete with professional looking engraving. It said:

BUSTER
1897-1910
BRAVEST DOG THAT EVER LIVED

Now I might not have known much about what life was like back in the early 1900's but I was pretty darn sure there weren't too many farm dogs from that era with their own granite tombstone or even wooden one, for that matter.

Bravest dog that ever lived...I tried to imagine what a dog could possibly do to deserve such high accolades. Wake the family as their house was burning down around them? Pull a near drowning victim to shore? Rescue Timmy from a well? Sure, any one of the three would have been a fine accomplishment for a dog to pull off, but brave? Brave enough to earn a tombstone nicer than most people had at the turn of the century? I didn't think so. I made a mental note to ask Mart about Buster and his bravery and went back to work.

Five minutes later I found the Christmas tree.

I was working my way down the edge of the yard toward the road when I heard a small, glassy 'pop' and felt something collapse and grate under the sole of my foot. Taking a step back to see what I'd stepped on, the sun's reflection suddenly flashed and danced across the mirrored surfaces of tiny thin shards of red, green, and silver glass. Getting back down on my knees, I positioned myself so the glass was in my shadow and tried to figure out what it was that I had inadvertently crushed.

The glass slivers were lying in a small oblong shape and were incredibly thin and brittle. Leaning over closer I carefully picked out the largest piece I could find and was just sitting back on my haunches to look it over when I noticed the cleanly cut, butt end of a small tree jutting out from under the thick canopy of weeds beyond my fingers. Tilting my head to get a better look, I saw more flashes of sun sparkles reflecting out from between the dry bare branches of the long dead tree. I looked back at the tiny piece of glass I was holding between my thumb and forefinger and my mind instantly made the connection. I had stepped on a Christmas tree ornament. Someone, almost certainly Mart, had thrown out a still decorated Christmas tree.

Moving slowly and cautiously, I cleared the weeds that were growing through, around, and over the naked skeleton of the abandoned tree, pulling out the different decorations I found as I went. After examining each one in turn I carefully laid each individual piece out on a bed of chopped weeds before going back for the next. I ended up crushing two more bulbs in spite of my efforts but by the time I was done I had three strings of the old style bulbous red and green Christmas tree bulbs, twenty-two delicate ornaments, a few cheesy plastic icicles, and the large intricately detailed glass angel from the top of the tree. While some of the ornaments were badly faded on one side from exposure to the sun, all of them had at least one good side and I carefully positioned each one with its brightest colors up. Compared to the plain-Jane round ornaments my mom and I used to decorate our imitation tree with out in California, these were beautiful; each one an absolute work of art.

Sitting back in the weeds, I tried to understand how Mart could have thrown out a fully decorated Christmas tree. These ornaments were old, delicate, and had to have been cared for by someone who loved and appreciated them, most probably Mart's wife. Throwing them away like so much garbage just didn't jibe with the mental image I had of the man's character. Throwing out something like his wife's Christmas ornaments sounded exactly like something my dad would do... something he would have *done* had mom not taken the Christmas decorations with us when we left for Detroit. As it turned out, it didn't really matter; mom didn't make it to the next Christmas anyway. She was killed in late November and I...

...and I left them there, packed away on the shelf in mom's bedroom.

The day before I was shipped back to California a lady from Social Services drove me over to the apartment to collect whatever I wanted to take back with me... and I didn't take mom's Christmas ornaments. In fact, I didn't take anything that belonged to my mom. Just looking at her things- her keys, her coffee cup, her toothbrush... even the new red Bic Lighter she had bought two or three days before she died just to see how it worked- just looking at the stuff she use to touch and wear and use every day and knowing she wasn't ever going to touch or wear or use any of those things ever again- seeing those things hurt me more than I could ever hope to explain. I didn't want any of those things; I wanted my mom! If I couldn't have her back I certainly didn't need any of her stuff around to remind me she was gone. At the time it seemed like the right thing to do- the only thing to do- but now, sitting out in the weeds of Mart's yard staring down at another dead woman's forgotten Christmas ornaments spread out on the ground under the hot summer sun, now I knew better.

I don't have many regrets in this life but I'll always wish I had taken something- anything- of my mom's to keep.

While I had no way of knowing when or how Mart's wife had died, I was suddenly certain that she had died right around Christmas. *My life ended when my wife died three years ago,* I remembered Mart saying before I walked out that first night. How long had they been married- fifty-five, sixty years? I couldn't even begin to put that many years into any kind of context. Sixty years was an eternity for me; how had Mart felt when the one person he had shared an eternity with had died and left him all alone?

Everyone's gone and everything has changed and I've been ready to die since I dropped that shovel of dirt on Mary's coffin.

The more I thought about the things Mart had said that night the more they bothered me. Even though I had been listening to him and heard everything he said, I was too preoccupied with my own little power struggle to see that he wasn't prattling along the way I assumed all old folks did when they had a captive audience. I didn't understand the magnitude of what he was telling me. I knew what it felt like to lose the most important person in your life and Mart had described it to a T. The only difference between the way the old man felt today and the way I felt after my mom died was I never <u>wanted</u> to die. Don't get me wrong; there were times I hurt so bad I felt like I <u>might</u> die but that was never what I wanted. I was young and there were about a million and a half things I had to do yet. My life was an unread book and I had to find out how it was going to turn out. Mart's book was old, tattered, and everything had been written except the last few pages... and he was tired of reading.

Of course Mart threw the Christmas tree out, what else could he do? I pictured him coming home after the funeral, walking into the house with the constant phantom pain of his missing wife jabbing at him everywhere he looked. I could see him sitting in his living room staring at the television set as it mindlessly spewed out whatever drivel happened to be playing, only he wasn't seeing Gilligan getting hit on the head with a coconut or Marshal Dillon strolling into the Longbranch... he was seeing his wife; thinking about how her carefully prepared body was lying in a cushioned casket under six feet of dirt and rock, alone and unprotected from the eternal silence that would always surround her, wishing he could get to her somehow and wondering how she could be so completely and irretrievably gone. The ghost of his wife must have been everywhere he looked in that house...but the sight of that Christmas tree would have been the worst. Not only was its presence in the house a symbol of all the other Christmas's they had shared over the years, but the pending chore of taking care of it by himself- wrapping up the lights, collecting the tinsel, and putting the different ornaments back in their boxes- that would have been the worst. And taking care of that stuff would have only been the first of a thousand steps in the insurmountable process of accepting her death. If it had been me I would have thrown the damn thing out too. And, like me, I thought it pretty likely that Mart had probably ended up regretting what he had done.

I looked around the sun-drenched yard and tried to figure out what to do. While I was pretty sure Mart would appreciate my finding the ornaments and saving them for him, I wasn't a hundred percent positive about it and I didn't want to take the risk of bringing them into the house where he was sure to come across them but I couldn't leave them where they were. I had to store them away somewhere and there was only one logical place to do that.

I made five trips back and forth out to the lower level of the barn and after looking around for a safe spot, I hid everything on the floor of the old car (a Ford Galaxie 500, I discovered after lifting the tarp enough to get the door open) Mart had stored out there.

That chore finished, I walked back out into the yard, tossed the feather light husk of the tree out into the weeds beyond the yard and went back to swinging my scythe.

My mind roamed as I worked. Something wasn't right. I'd started out the morning feeling like I was on top of the world, the day ahead bursting with possibility and promise, but now...now a vague sense of doom seemed to be lurking just around the corner. It wasn't hiding, this nagging feeling of dread. It had something to do with the Christmas tree and the dog cemetery I'd found under the weeds, whether one or both I wasn't sure.

Mart's truck chugged up the driveway and rolled to a stop in a cloud of dust. Climbing out, Mart walked back to the bed, lifted out a small gas can and set it down in the shade of the pine tree.

"Still here, eh?" he called out as I walked up to his truck.

"Yes, sir," I smiled.

"How'd the gloves work out for you?" he asked as we started for the house. "Notice any difference, did you?"

"World of difference," I answered. "They worked great."

Mart led the way up the stairs and onto the porch. Standing on the deck, he turned and surveyed the yard.

"Looks like you're really going to town on those weeds, son."

Unaccustomed to receiving compliments, I didn't know what to say.

"I found something out there I wanted to ask you about," I said, changing the subject.

Mart turned and started to say something but stopped. The change in his manner was obvious and I suddenly knew I'd made the right choice in taking the ornaments out to the barn.

"What'd you find, boy?" he asked quietly, looking back off toward the spot where I'd found the Christmas tree.

"Well, I guess you'd call it your dog cemetery," I said, doing my best to act like I hadn't noticed the way he'd tightened up. "I was wondering if you could tell me what Buster did to get such a nice tombstone."

The guarded look in Mart's eyes faded and his expression immediately softened.

"My God," he said, shaking his head, "You do take your work seriously, don't you, son."

I looked at the old man, not at all sure what he was talking about.

"Those graves are tucked away in the far corner of the yard," he explained. "Hedging the corners a little would have been the easiest thing in the world to do- nothing more than human nature, I guess- and you'd have saved yourself quite a little bit of swinging in the process."

I cringed as I figured out I was getting another compliment. Mart must have noticed he was making me uncomfortable.

"So you want to hear about old Buster, do you?" he said. "Well let's go on inside so I can rustle up a cup of coffee for myself and maybe a pop for you and then I'll tell you how that dog ended up with a hundred dollar tombstone."

Mart turned and, after taking one more quick glance out to the far edge of the yard, led the way inside.

"Now I might as well start off by telling you this right out of the gate," Mart said, sitting down at the table with his coffee. "Buster never did anything to earn that inscription on his headstone. He was always a good dog and I've no doubt he would have died to protect me had the opportunity presented itself, but it never did come to that. Buster lived a good long life for a dog and he died the way a lot of animals do when they know it's their time; he laid down in a quiet spot and died alone."

Mart paused and took a sip of his coffee.

"You ever had a dog, boy?" he asked, setting the cup down carefully.

"No sir," I answered. I started to add something but stopped. I didn't want the old man to think I was weird.

"What?" he said. "You had some other kind of pet, did you?"

I studied my Coke can for a minute.

(It was our first night in a new apartment- a night that always felt kind of unsettling no matter how many times we moved- and I couldn't sleep. I kept hearing noises; little squeaks and rustlings that always stopped as soon as I turned on the light...)

"I had a pet mouse for awhile," I said.

"Is that right," Mart said, talking as if a mouse were a perfectly normal choice for a pet. "What kind of mouse? One of those white ones?"

(I started off by naming him Mr. Whiskers and leaving little offerings of table scraps next to the wall behind the dresser. A week later he was eating out of my hand. Two weeks after that he was running out to greet me when I walked into my room.)

"Just a regular house mouse," I said.

I very nearly added the scientific name Mus musculus (I'd gone to the library to see what exactly I should be feeding Mr. Whiskers and had noticed the term in parenthesis under the disappointingly pedestrian name of House Mouse, which was beneath the picture of a mouse that could have been Mr. Whisker's twin) but just managed to catch myself in time. It might have taken me awhile but I had finally come to realize that one of the main reasons my dad didn't like me was because I always seemed to be spouting off about little know-it-all shit like that whenever dad tried to talk to me about anything beyond the realm of which direction the rabbit ears had to be positioned to pick up channel six. While he never really came right out and told me so, the disgusted, tight-lipped glare that flittered across his face whenever I used a term like cumulus clouds or schizophrenia- that jaundiced flash of contempt and anger that flared in his eyes whenever I tried to prove to him I was smart enough to be worthy of his attention- those momentary flashes of naked repugnance never failed to hit their mark and hobble my already clumsy attempts to please him. The thought of seeing a look like that ripple across Mart's face scared me badly.

"I didn't have him very long," I said. "He ended up getting stepped on."

Stomped on would have been the more correct term. Mr. Whiskers made the mistake of running out to greet my mom one day when she walked into my room with some laundry. Mom wasn't afraid of mice but she did associate them with sickness and disease and had wasted no time in sending Mr. Whiskers to mouse heaven. I came home from school just as she was flushing him down the toilet.

"One of your folks squash him, did they?" Mart

asked and I jumped a little in my chair. I was honestly beginning to think the old man could read my mind.

"How'd you know that?" I demanded.

"Same thing happened to me," Mart smiled. "Or something pretty similar anyway. I found a whole litter of mouse pups out next to the barn one day when I was just a little tyke and decided to adopt them. My ma found 'em nestled in a tin under my bed the next day and had my daddy throw 'em into the cook stove."

"Ah, geeze," I winced.

"Oh, yeah," Mart nodded. "I remember I cried and begged him not to do it and ended up getting a swat for my trouble. It was a bad day for me all right but if it weren't for those little pups getting burned up in the stove that day I doubt I'd have ever been able to keep Buster." Mart took another sip of his coffee, sat back in his chair and crossed his legs.

"We ended up getting Buster the same way most folks came by their dogs back when I was a boy; he just wandered into the yard one day. According to the way my folks always told the story, my ma looked out the kitchen window one day to check on me- I guess I couldn't have been but five or so at the time- and there I was, playing with a strange dog. And I don't mean strange as in I was playing with a dog she had never seen before, though that's exactly what Buster was at the time. No, what I'm saying is this; the dog just looked downright goofy. His head was about four sizes too big for his small to middlin' sized body, his dirty yellow fur looked and felt like pig hair only thicker and longer, except for the hair on his tail which was soft and white, and his eye- he only had one, having lost the other to a stick or animal sometime before he showed up- always looked to be on the verge of bugging right out of his skull. Every farm dog you ever saw back in those days was of the Heinz 57 variety but let me tell you what, Buster had 'em all beat when it came to the uglies.

"Martin Jonas, you get away from that animal!' ma yelled out the window as soon as she caught sight of that dog. Now according to the way the story was always told, I supposedly yelled right back at my ma and sassed her. I don't actually remember ma having anything to do with how things turned out with Buster that day so I can't really say yea or nay on whether or not that's true but I can tell you this; if I did sass ma like the story goes I would have got the strap when daddy came home that night and I know that didn't happen. I was on the receiving end of that strap twice in my life and I remember both times just as clear as a bell so I think there may have been some artistic license taken over the years.

"'No!' I supposedly yelled back at ma. 'This here's my dog and his name's Buster. He told me so.'

"Now here again, common sense and what supposedly happened that day seem to part company. According to the story my ma always told, she was shocked speechless by my sassing back at her and she just let me go about my business, thinking she'd let my daddy show me the error of my ways when he got in that night. You never knew my ma, of course, but let me tell you, son, she was one woman who was never at a loss for words once you got her dander up. Why, ma could stop the rain if it riled her to have it falling; her letting me get away with being too big for my britches like that doesn't sound like something she would ever do, but who knows? My folks were both honest to a fault so there must be a grain of truth in there somewhere...or maybe that's exactly what happened, I don't know. This next part though, I remember.

Mart lit another cigarette, slid the Zippo back into his pocket and ran a hand over the top of his head.

"My daddy was always a fair and reasonable man who never swatted you unless you had it coming,' he started slowly, "but he was also a hard man who never had any use for an animal that couldn't pull his own weight around the farm and I can't say as I blame him for being that way. I had five older brothers and sisters who lived long enough to be counted as such, plus ma and then her ma after grandpa died while putting his boots on one morning, and providing for that many mouths back in those days wasn't something to be taken lightly. If an animal couldn't be sold or harnessed or eaten it had no business on daddy's farm and I knew it. Five minutes after I found Buster- or five minutes after he found me more likely- I was trying to come up with a reason to give my daddy to keep him from shooting my new dog when he got home that night. Buster and I talked it over, or at least I imagined we did which is pretty damn close for a five-year-old, and we finally hit on something. When daddy came walking up to the house that evening Buster and I were both waiting for him on the porch steps. I stood up and started in on him before he had a chance to say boo.

"Daddy,' I said just as big as life, 'this here is my dog Buster. He's the bravest dog in the whole world so you'd better not go shooting him.'

"Now this was serious business to me, of course, but I guess daddy had one hell of a time keeping a straight face. There I was, standing tall at three foot nothing, my chest all puffed out and looking just as serious as a heart attack... and then there was Buster, bravest dog in the world, crouched down between my feet, staring up at him with that one bulging eye, scared to death and piddling on the stoop.

"Bravest dog in the world, eh?' daddy said when he was able. 'You sure about that, son?'

"'Yes sir,' I shot back. 'I been watching him all day and he ain't afraid of nothing; he's awful brave alright.'

"Well daddy looked down at that big headed, pig haired, one eyed dog sitting there in a puddle of his own water and he knew he wasn't looking at any thing much as far as dog flesh went, but- and I wouldn't hear this part until after Mary and I started having babies ourselves- he had always felt bad about the way he'd tossed those little pups into the stove right in front of me that day and he'd been trying to find a way to make up for it. I guess his pa had done something similar to him when he was just a little guy and he, that is to say my daddy, was never able to forgive him for doing it.

"'I knew I couldn't undo what I'd done,' daddy told me one day years later while the two of us were watching my oldest playing out in the field with his dog. 'All I could do was hope that letting you keep that ugly little dog might help balance the scales a bit back in my favor.'"

Mart started to raise his cigarette to his mouth, noticed it had gone out and tossed it in the ashtray.

"Did it help?" I asked. "Did you forgive your dad for burning up your mice?"

"Oh, sure," Mart nodded. "But it didn't have anything to do with him letting me keep Buster. My daddy and his pa were two completely different men, you see. My daddy never meant to hurt any of us kids; he might have made a mistake or two along the way, I don't know that there's a father who hasn't, but you always knew he had a good heart and he was only trying to do what was right. I'm afraid daddy couldn't say the same when it came to the way his father treated him. He never said too much about his pa but from what I gathered over the years ol' Zebedia Ash was a man who liked his whisky and he was always one ornery son of a bitch whether he had a bottle in his hand or not."

The old man went about the business of lighting another cigarette.

"But your dad turned out alright though, huh?" I asked. "Even with a son of a bitch for a dad, he turned out okay?"

Mart looked at me over his cigarette as he snapped the Zippo closed. He took his time putting the lighter back into his pocket.

"You know anything at all about farming, son?"

Confused by the question, I shook my head.

"Well, it's gotten to be quite a bit more complicated over the last few years, what with fertilizers, insecticides and hybrid seeds and such, but back when I started farming the one main thing I had to worry about was the rain. Not enough of it and our crops could end up stunted or, if it got real bad, they'd wither up and die. Too much and we'd lose everything planted in the low areas and mold would cut into what was left. Most years everything would work out all right; it'd be too wet or too dry for a week or two but things would even out over time and we'd usually end up with enough of a harvest to make a buck or two and still have enough to feed the family over the winter. Now I can see I've lost you here but just hang in there for another second or two and I'll make my point.

"One year, 1937 this was, we had us a picture perfect spring around here. Every day from May to the end of June was just as sunny and calm as a man could ever hope for. No storms, no frost, nothing but warm sunny days and, more often than not, an easy spring rain at night.

"Everything I planted that year grew like a house a'fire; wheat and hay were both looking to be ready for their first cutting by the beginning of July, cornstalks were up to my chin, and Mary's vegetable garden looked like a jungle. Every farmer knows better than to count his harvest before it's stowed or sold, but that's exactly what I was doing that year. The way things were going I figured we were looking at clearing better than a thousand dollar profit that fall, more money than this farm had ever mustered in any three years before then combined. I thought I'd died and gone to farmer's heaven.

"Well, we got our first real thunderstorm that year on the last night in June. It really wasn't much as far as storms go, just your run of the mill summer squall and a light one at that. I remember waking up as it blew in that night but I didn't even bother getting out of bed. There wasn't any hail, the wind was blowing along at a pretty good clip but not hard enough to whistle through the eves the way it would if it were really set on cranking up, and the rain, what little we got, was light and misty on the windows. Things could have changed of course- they'll do that once in a while, start off easy and then work themselves up to a real humdinger- so I laid awake and listened until it played itself out and then I drifted off to sleep thinking about the new tractor I was going to buy that fall.

"The next morning I stepped out of the house to find we'd lost damn near everything. If I hadn't heard the storm with my own ears I would have thought a tornado had come along and set up housekeeping during the night. Eighty acres of corn we had that year and every stalk was either broken off clean or lying flat with the root ball pulled right up out of the ground. The hay and wheat fields fared a mite better, but not much, and Mary's garden looked like some kind of giant thing had come along and stepped on it. And it wasn't just us; every farm within ten miles of here was in the same boat. All told this farm ended up losing three quarters of the harvest I'd been spending in my head that spring and no one could tell me why.

"I guess it took about a week before the boys down to the Grange got together and brought some college kid up from the University of Michigan's Agriculture Extension to check things out and this is the just of what he finally told us:

"The perfect spring we had that year was just a little too perfect. Our crops hadn't ever experienced any stress, you see... they didn't have any backbone. No drought, no wind, no cold, they had no experience in dealing with neglect or hardship and that was the reason they had grown so big and tall so fast... and that was the reason they all came down at the drop of a hat. They hadn't ever been tested by anything stronger than a light shower that spring and when something stronger came along, well, they just couldn't stand up to it. They didn't know how.

"Now I could be wrong but I've always thought that same principle might apply to people just the same as it did to those crops back in '37. You asked if my daddy turned out all right in spite of having an ornery son of a bitch for a father and I guess my answer to that would have to be no. I think it far more likely that he turned out all right <u>because</u> of his father. My daddy had a rough go in life when he was a boy, that's true enough, but I believe he ended up the better man because of it, you see? He'd made it through more than his share of hardship and neglect and he went on to thrive. He could have taken an easier path and slid through life on the backs of others like his pa always tried to do, but he didn't. He abided his pa. He watched and he learned from him, even though the man never meant to teach him a thing."

Mart paused. I could see he was expecting me to say something but this subject was hitting just a little too close to home to suit me.

"Oh," I said.

I thought I might have seen a look of disappointment in Mart's eyes but it passed quickly, if it had been there at all.

"Well for what it's worth, that's always been my theory," Mart went on without missing a beat. "It might not apply to every kid, I know Mary and I did everything we could to see that our children had it better than we did when we were growing up and none of them ever gave us any reason to regret it, but there's always exceptions to every rule. Some kids just seem destined to turn out bad no matter if their folks are saints or sinners or somewhere in between. In the end I think it's mostly up to the kid to decide for himself."

Mart leaned over the table and butted his cigarette out in the ashtray.

"Now where was I before I jumped the track?" he asked, sitting back and scowling a little.

"You were just saying your dad let you keep Buster," I prompted.

"That's right," Mart nodded. "Daddy let me keep Buster that day and, like I said, he was always a good dog. I learned a lot from him."

That struck me as odd, the old man saying he learned a lot from his dog. I pictured a kid and his dog sitting in the dirt with the dog scratching out 2 + 2 = 4 on the ground with his paw and smiled.

"Now don't be so quick to judge there, boy," Mart said, squinting a disapproving eye at me. "You say you've never had a dog yourself so there's no way for you to know what it is that I'm talking about here. Buster was special, I'll grant you that- why, all I had to do was look at him sometimes and he could tell what I was thinking- but I can guarantee you this; you'll never find a human as understanding or loyal or forgiving as a found dog can be if you give him just half a chance. Oh, a man can learn a lot of things from a dog, that's a fact; things that can't be taught or learned any other way except by experiencing them and then using your God-given common sense to understand what it is you've learned, a quality most folks seem to lack these days. I've had seven different dogs in my life and I've always been able to learn a little something from each one of them, but Buster was the one that taught me the most. The only thing I regret is I didn't understand what I was learning until after he died."

The old man shifted in his chair, cleared his throat and looked out the kitchen window. He didn't say anything for a good minute.

"Buster used to walk me to school every day I had to go," he said wonderingly. "I don't care if it was hot, cold, raining or snowing; if I had to go to school, Buster went too. He couldn't go in, of course, but he was there, out in the yard if it was nice or curled up under the porch if it was cold or raining, and there he'd wait until I came back out.

Twenty-some kids would come flying out of that school at the end of the day but Buster didn't see any of them but me. He'd run up and greet me like I'd been gone for a year or more, tail wagging and jumping around like it was a miracle I'd made it out of the old Standard School alive... and half the time I wouldn't even notice him there- I'd be too busy talking with Joe Kelly or Johnny Oberson or making eyes at Olive Sockavich to pay him any mind, sometimes I wouldn't even pet him or ruffle his fur, but Buster didn't care. He wasn't there because he had to be; he was there because he loved me more than anyone else ever did in this world except for maybe my ma and Mary. He wanted to be there because I was his boy and he was my dog. He waited there in that schoolyard every day from my first day in school to the day I graduated, and the only thing I ever did to repay his loyalty was to take it for granted. It wasn't until after he went off and laid down for the last time that I understood the depth and width of that dog's love for me and by then it was too late for me to tell him I was sorry; sorry for all the times I ignored him or hollered at him for nothing more than wanting my attention. It was too late to tell him I hadn't been worthy of the love he had always had for me."

Mart leaned forward, pulled a calico handkerchief from his back pocket and gave his nose a couple of quick perfunctory honks. The old man was crying! He wasn't making a big production out of it, I wouldn't even have known if I hadn't been looking directly at him and noticed the tears well up in his eyes before being channeled and absorbed amongst the lines of age that marked his face. But the old man was crying and it wasn't because he was drunk and having a pity party for himself. He was crying over a dog that had been dead for over 60 years!

"I learned a hard lesson when Buster died, oh yes I did," he went on as he stuffed the handkerchief back into his pocket, "but it was a lesson I took to heart and never forgot- a lesson that saved me from a grief I can only imagine after

Mary and I lost little Joan and August to the flu in '18. God might not have saw fit to let us have them very long- Joan was five and August was but two days past his fourth birthday- but we had them long enough for me to see and recognize that look of unconditional love I'd seen once before in an ugly yellow dog, and thanks to him I knew enough to never take that love for granted. I guess part of me died right along with those kids when we buried them that day but at least I had the satisfaction of knowing neither of them had ever known a day their father hadn't told them how much he loved them, and knowing that still means more to me than you can ever imagine."

Staring out the window and off into the past, Mart lapsed into silence as a muted wind rustled through the isolated old farmhouse. The birds sang and the clock ticked and the world steadfastly revolved a few more degrees toward the future.

"You haven't seen it yet," Mart went on a while later, "but there's a little lake out past the field beyond the barn. Buster and I spent a lot of time back there when I was a boy, fishing, mostly, but sometimes we'd just sit in the shade against the trunk of our favorite tree and watch the loons and the ducks and the muskrats... and that's where Buster went when it was his time to die. I found him out there, curled up in the spot that was his next to our tree. I sat there with him for a while and then I carried him back up to the house, buried him over there in the corner of the yard, and then I marked his grave with a plain wooden cross.

"Daddy was the one that bought the headstone you see out there today. It was a hundred dollar headstone just like I said, but daddy got it for the price of the engraving- a dollar and a quarter- on account of it had been dropped off the wagon and broken by the boys who used to deliver the stones up from Grand Rapids. I don't know how daddy ever heard about it but Mr. Piechell, he was the undertaker back then, was using it as a stepping stone for his outhouse. He told daddy he could have it for nothing just as long as it was for a dog and didn't end up marking a person's grave up to the cemetery. So daddy went ahead and dug it up, cleaned it off and had Piechell do the engraving. He was the one who decided to add 'Bravest Dog in the World'... said he'd never been able to look at Buster and me without that phrase coming to mind and he thought it to be a damn fine epitaph.

"The two of us spent the better part of a summer's day settin' that stone in a bed of clay we hauled up from the creek bed, but by the time we were done you couldn't even tell the thing had been broken; all you could see was a fine little crack running right down between the dates."

"It sure didn't look broken to me." I said.

Mart nodded and smiled.

"That's daddy's work for you," he said. "Sixty-four years and it still looks as good as the day he set it. Daddy might have been a farmer by trade but he could always do anything he set his mind to. Why, he and ma bought this property for fifty cents an acre just after the loggers finished it off back in 1879- a copy of the deed hangs there in the living room if you haven't noticed it yet- and by the time I came along thirteen years later, he'd pulled eighty acres worth of stumps, built the barn that sits out back, built this very house we're sitting in, and he managed to keep his family fed at the same time. He did it all with nothing more than his own two hands and the sweat of his brow.

"He was a quiet man, daddy was. Oh, he might have talked up ma or maybe one or the other of us kids from time to time but he sure wasn't one to crow over anything he'd done himself. A lot of pride went into everything he did but that's right where it stayed; the house still stands, barn still stands, his mark is still visible on the land he tilled, and he did it all without any expectation of praise. He was always comfortable in his own skin, he was, and I'll tell you what I mean. I heard him take a lot of ribbing about Buster's headstone over the years from a few of the other old boys who farmed around here but never once did he offer up an explanation to any one of them. He'd listen to their smart-ass remarks about how nice it must be to be rich enough to buy a headstone for a scrawny little no-account dog and he'd just stand there nodding, taking whatever they wanted to dish out. Then, after the subject had been worn out and dropped and old Jimmy O'Mally or Freddy Hamner or whoever had been doing the ribbin' went on to other matters, daddy'd catch my eye, smile a little with his so as no one else could see him doing it, and he'd tip me a wink. We both knew he hadn't put that headstone out there for Buster's sake, you see; he'd done it for me and he didn't have to say a word to anyone else to justify having done it."

Taking the last sip of his coffee, Mart looked over at me and shook his head.

"Listen to me talk, would you," he said. "Why, I haven't strung that many words together since Hector was a pup." Pushing himself up from his chair, the old man arched his back and walked over to the sink.

"Well," he said as he turned on the spigot and began to rinse out the cup, "I guess I might have taken the long way around in telling it, but that's the story behind Buster and his headstone. 'Course there's a story or two behind every marker you see out there but I think I've done about enough story telling for one day."

"Why don't you have a dog now?" I asked. Hadn't this been the question I'd wanted to ask all along? According to what Mart had said the first day I met him he'd been living alone for over three years and he never got any company. Why didn't he have a dog now?

"Your last dog, Mindy; she died over five years ago, didn't she?"

"Yes she did," Mart nodded. Shutting off the water, he placed the cup sideways in the drain tray next to the sink and started back toward the table.

"Well five years is a long time," I pushed. "Why didn't you replace her? It seems like having a dog around would be a lot better than being alone every day."

"You don't 'replace' one dog with another, son," Mart said, sitting back down in his chair. "You might as well ask me why I didn't run out and replace Mary after she died."

Mart was doing his best to sidestep my question but I needed an answer. I kept my mouth shut and waited him out.

"Wouldn't be fair to the dog," he finally said.

"What do you mean?" I asked. "What wouldn't be fair about you getting another dog?"

"I mean I'm an old man, son," he said defensively. "It'd be selfish of me to take in another dog when I'm this close to the grave. Dogs are supposed to die before their owners, not the other way around."

"Well, what about an older dog?" I asked desperately. "Maybe you could go to the pound and pick out-"

"I'm too old, boy," Mart said forcibly. "Too old to take on the responsibility of another dog and that's all there is to it. I've lived too long as it is; why, having a dog around would just give me a reason-"

Mart stopped, a look of realization dawning in his eyes, but it was too late. I had my answer. Having a dog around would have just given the old man a reason to live... and he didn't want that.

I looked down at my hands and blinked back the hot tears that threatened to give me away. I couldn't stay here. If Mart didn't want a dog around he sure as hell wasn't interested in taking in a fourteen year old boy.

"You know I don't get it," I said. I looked up and a single tear got away and coursed down my cheek as I glared at the old man.

"If God really wanted you to help me like you said

he did, why didn't he just let you die instead of my mom?"

"Listen, son-" Mart started, but I wasn't having any of it. I got up, walked across the floor and out the door.

Mart didn't say a word to try and stop me.

I trotted across the yard over to where I had left the scythe, picked it up and started swinging.

If I had to pick the point in my life where I was closest to losing whatever that one quality is in a person that pushes him on to remain true to his hopes and dreams and aspirations, to remain true to himself regardless of the pain or cost, this would have been it. I was ready to give up.

Starting over every few months in a strange school, Cindy getting kicked out of the house, my parents divorce, the sterile, aloof, and ultimately nonexistent relationship with my dad, mom dying; everything I had endured and fought and survived in my life had somehow been resurrected by my coming here and now I was expected to take them all on at once. I just couldn't do it, not by myself. I was tired of fighting for something I'd never in my life known anyone to possess.

Mart wanted to die.

I couldn't understand it.

The old man brought out a sandwich and a Coke a while later. I was working my way across the yard when I noticed him walking up out of the corner of my eye and I changed course just enough to keep my back to him.

"Hungry?"

I swung the scythe a couple more times before stopping. Running my hand back through my hair, I tossed the tool off to one side and turned around. Mart held out a can of pop and a sandwich wrapped up in a paper towel. Peeling off my gloves, I sauntered over and took them from him.

"Thanks." I tossed the word out like a piece of trash.

I knew what the old man had come to sell and I wasn't buying. He wanted to die, end of story. Oh, I'd listen to whatever it was he had to say; I'd nod in all the right places and let him believe whatever it was he wanted to believe, but I was leaving anyway. I'd finish the yard first, I wanted him to see that at least one of us was a man of his word, but after that you could color me gone, gone, gone. I knew turning my back on him would hurt him (in spite of his desire to die, I was pretty sure Mart honestly thought he wanted to do whatever he could to help me) and that was exactly what I was looking for; I wanted to hurt him. I was tired of always being the one to get the dirty end of the stick in every deal and I figured it was about time I started doling out a little comeuppance. I wanted to be the bad guy for once. I had taken a huge risk in allowing myself to trust Mart, he had gotten closer to me in three days than my father ever did in the fourteen years I'd known him, but in the end the old man had let me down just like everybody else.

Sitting down on a stump, I unwrapped the sandwich, set it on my knee and popped opened the Coke. Let the apologies commence. I took a bite of my sandwich and chewed while I waited. Trying to appear nonchalant, I glanced over to the spot where Mart had been standing when I sat down but he wasn't there. Surprised, I looked up toward the house just in time to see him take the last couple steps across the porch to the door and walk back inside. He never looked back.

The anger I'd been nursing for the last couple hours drained away as I stared at the house, trying to understand what had just happened.

After a while, I turned back to my lunch and ate alone.

It was nearly dark and every weed in the yard had fallen to my scythe by the time I quit for the day. I'd been tempted to knock off earlier but the thought of having to face Mart when I went in had kept me going. I knew now I'd been acting like a jackass that afternoon and I owed him an apology.

Standing out next to the road where I had finished, I lit up a cigarette and looked the yard over. It looked a lot better than it had before I started but it was still a long way from looking like a lawn. Tomorrow I'd pick up the weeds with a wheelbarrow I'd noticed out in the barn, haul them away, and mow down the stubble left behind. With any luck I'd be done before dark and be ready to head for Grand Rapids early the next day. I wasn't looking forward to leaving (I'd already decided I'd never live in the city a minute longer than I absolutely had to) and I wasn't doing it to hurt Mart... not anymore. It was just something I knew I had to do.

I could see now that it wasn't Mart's fault I had been disappointed with his answer to my thinly veiled question; hadn't he told me right up front he'd been ready, willing, and waiting to die since the day he lost his wife? Hadn't he told me that that was the reason he wanted to help me in the first place, so he could die? And wouldn't an older kid, a smarter kid, have picked up on the other, more subtle ways he had of saying the same thing; the heavy smoking, not eating enough to keep a bird alive, the way he had let everything around him go to pot... what else could he have done to make me understand? He'd only known me for three days, for God's sake, how could he have even known there was a need to make me understand? He didn't know the first thing about me, I had made sure of that, how had I ever convinced myself I had a right to even hope he'd let me stay?

Mart didn't have anything left to live for and he didn't <u>want</u> anything to live for. All he wanted to do was keep a forgotten promise he'd made to God so he could die.

Who was I to say he was wrong? It didn't make any sense to me, this desire to die, but then I was just a kid; what did I know about getting old?

I looked up to the house and saw the silhouette of the old man through the kitchen window. He was sitting at the table with his back to me, smoking. I watched him for a while, trying to imagine what he was thinking, what he was feeling, what he was remembering. I wanted to help him somehow, give him part of whatever it was I had in my soul that made me want to get up in the morning and live another day. I wanted to make him curious again, remind him what it was to wonder and hope and dream. But even as I wished for these things, I knew Mart wouldn't want them. The only thing life had to offer him now was his death. Knowing that, even though I'd only met the man three days earlier, hurt me more than I can describe.

Better to cut my losses now and get on with my life.

I stopped at the top of the porch steps and peered into the house through the rusty screen door. Mart was still sitting at the table but I could see now that he wasn't just sitting there; he was looking at some kind of huge book. Feeling like a peeping tom, I stood where I was and watched him, not sure I wanted to intrude. Mart worked his way down to the bottom of the page he was on and then turned it, handling the thick yellowed paper carefully. I saw a wink of dull silvery light refracted from three or four glossy surfaces adhered to the page and realized the old man was looking at a photo album. Knowing he was probably looking at pictures of dead people he had once known didn't make me feel any better about walking in but what choice did I have? I had to face him sooner or later, and besides, the mosquitoes were about to eat me alive.

"Knock, knock," I said quietly.

Mart glanced up at the door, saw it was me, and looked back down at his pictures. Not a very promising sign. I opened the screen door and stepped inside, waiting to catch the door to keep it from slapping against the frame.

"You had me wondering, boy," Mart said without looking up. "Thought you might just work the night straight through out there."

"I decided to try and get all the weeds down by dark," I answered self-consciously. I walked across the mudroom floor and stepped into the kitchen. "Just barely made it."

"Good for you," Mart nodded, still looking down at the album.

I stood just inside the entrance and waited. I had hoped to get right to it and apologize for the way I had acted that afternoon but I wasn't sure how to interpret the way the old man was acting. I decided it might be better to just start off slow and work my way up to it.

"I'm pretty sure the yard will only take me another day," I said. "I'll haul the weeds away first thing in the morning and then all I'll have left to do is the mowing."

Preoccupied with his pictures, Mart nodded without looking up and turned another page.

"Unless there's something else you really need me to do around here before I go, I guess I'll be leaving after that's done."

Mart slowly lifted his head and looked at me for what seemed like a long time. I felt my face flush but I didn't look away; I was only doing what was best for both of us and I refused to let myself feel guilty. Mart finally looked back down to the photo album without saying anything.

"There's something else," I took a step closer to the table. "I-I owe you an apology for -"

"I've always loved this picture of Mary," Mart interrupted quietly, gazing down at the photo album.

I stopped, a little taken aback. Mart was too preoccupied with the picture to notice.

"The preacher hadn't pronounced us man and wife more than an hour or so before this was taken," he said. "You can't see me in this but I was standing right over here," the old man pointed a blunt fingertip to a spot an inch or so away from the right edge of the photograph. "We'd only planned on getting one wedding picture taken that day, one of the two of us in our fancy clothes, and we couldn't hardly afford that, but then, after the photographer took that one picture of the two of us, he looked over at me and asked if I was sure I didn't want just one more picture, maybe a nice portrait of my wife by herself." Mart smiled and shook his head.

"My wife," he said wonderingly. "God, I can still remember how...how different that sounded to me. I must have heard that phrase a thousand times before that day but it had never applied to me, to us, before. My wife. Hearing that photographer call Mary my wife made it official somehow; it meant more coming out of his mouth than when the preacher said it from the pulpit. I looked at Mary and she looked at me, her eyes just a'sparkling like they are here in this picture, and I knew she was thinking the same thing. I told the man I thought a portrait of my wife sounded like a fine idea and I stepped off to the side there. The photographer got set up again, ducked under the cloth, and just as he got ready to push the plunger, I leaned forward and whispered, 'Smile, Mrs. Ash.' Well, I'd no more than got that out than Mary started to turn to look at me and that's when the photographer took this picture... a second later and he'd have caught the back of her head. Cost me a buck and a quarter to have him take this picture back then but it was money well spent; having it now means more to me than all the money in the world."

Mart trailed off as his eyes wandered longingly over photograph. I just stood where I was, not completely sure he even remembered I was there.

Looking up as if he'd heard my thoughts, Mart sat up and carefully slid the album around on the table to face me.

"Take a look, son," he said, tilting his head to admire the photograph as I walked over to the table. "Wasn't she something?"

The photograph was an 8x10 tintype; the glassy surface wavered under the kitchen light as I approached, quivering between a bright negative image to a sharply lined but deeply shadowed black and white photograph. It was nestled in the very center of the page, matted between heavy sheets of thick, cumbersome tan paper with the words 'My Wedding Day' written in a feminine hand beneath. A dusty, settled odor of decomposing paper and glue enveloped me as I leaned over the table to look at the woman who's death had taken her husband's will to live.

She was holding a bouquet of wildflowers, their colors lost to the clumsiness of the black and white plate. The stark white of her simple wedding dress had faded to gray, her skin to a coppery gold. The background was the inside of a church, a roughly hewn cross hung from the plain wood planks that made up the wall beyond her shoulder. The posture of her body was self-conscious and posed and unremarkable. Everything about the photograph was dark, antiquated, and somehow sad... everything except for the face of whom it had been taken.

She was so young.

The beauty of her youth and innocence transcended the limitations of the photograph, the luminous expression of her unaffected love and happiness still evident in the tilt of her chin, the arch of her brow, the curve of a growing secret smile. Her eyes were bright and aware, mischievously surprised and turning- the camera eye forgotten- to look to the only man (*my husband!*) for whom this shared expression of love was ever intended. She was every boy's dream, every parent's hope, every man's desire. Staring down at her from a time she would never know, my heart ached at the loss.

"She's beautiful," I breathed.

"Yes she was," Mart nodded. Sitting back in his chair, he lit a cigarette and crossed his legs.

"You know it's funny," he said, taking his time with his thought. "Before Mary died, I used to wake up in the night from time to time and worry about what might happen if I were to die before she did. I'd lie there for hours sometimes, scared to death at the thought of leaving her alone. I'd watch her sleep and imagine the different things that could happen to her, not terrible things mind you, but conceivable things... sad, lonely things that a younger man would never imagine ever happening to his wife, and I'd plead with God to let me be the one that got left behind if he couldn't see fit to take us both at the same time. Of course, the idea of Mary dying before I did scared me too. We'd never spent a night apart, right up until the end, but the thought of her grieving, of being old and alone, that scared me more. I knew, or at least I thought I knew, that it'd be best if I were the one left behind when the time came... and that's the way I felt right up to the minute she died. She'd been so tired and so sick for so long that I'd actually come to believe it would be a blessing when God got around to calling her home, but it turned out I was wrong about that, too, I'd never been so wrong about anything in my life. The best part of me died right along with Mary that night and the rest of me just gave up. Mary never would have done that; she was always one to see the best things in life and she was a fighter. Mary would have gone on living."

The house was silent except for the faint ticking of the clock. I thought back to finding the skeletal remains of Mart's Christmas tree that morning. Had I honestly thought I had any concept of the pain the old man felt over his wife?

"You don't plan on leaving here without telling me first, do you, son?" Mart asked.

"No sir," I answered, surprised at the question. "Why?"

Mart shrugged. Tucking his cigarette in his mouth, he reached out for the photo album and slid it back around to look at his wife's picture. It was pretty obvious he'd rather be left alone.

"Well," I said, straightening up and arching my back, "I guess I'll take a shower." Mart nodded without looking up.

I started for the bathroom, walking slowly and

looking at the old man. He looked lost and beaten. I wanted to help him but I didn't know how.

Putting his cigarette out in the ashtray, Mart sighed as he closed the photo album.

"I'm going for a drive, boy," he said, glancing over at me as he stood. Picking up the album, he carried it into his bedroom. A second later he came back out and started toward the door.

"I'll be back," he said.

"You want me to go with you?" I asked. Halfway across the kitchen floor, Mart slowed and then stopped before looking at me.

"I appreciate the offer, son," Mart said gently, "but I'm afraid I wouldn't be very good company tonight."

"Oh," I said. "All right."

Mart turned and walked out of the room. I heard the screen door creak as he pushed it open.

"I think you were right," I called.

I waited, expecting to hear the screen door slam as a response but the sound never came. Taking a step over to the entrance of the mudroom, I saw the old man standing in the doorway with his back to me, his arm holding the door.

"I think you were right about God sending me here," I said. "But I don't think he sent me here for you to take care of me, not any more."

Mart didn't turn around but he didn't walk away either.

"I appreciate all the things you've done for me, buying me clothes and stuff and letting me stay here, but I don't think that's why God put me on a bus and shipped me three thousand miles across the country. I think he sent me here to listen to you.

"I've learned things from you, things I think I needed to know before it was too late for me to believe they mattered, things most people don't seem to know or don't want to know, things no one else ever could have told me...and even if someone had tried, I never would have listened. Hell, I didn't want to listen to you, remember? I must have walked ten miles after I left that first night but I still ended up right back here where I'd started. I think everything that happened to bring me here happened because God knew I'd never have sat still long enough to listen to anybody else but you.

"You don't need to feel bad about me leaving, Mr. Ash, I'll be okay now. You've kept your promise to God and I'm sure he knows it."

The old man stood in the doorway, looking out into the night.

"Thank you, son," he whispered.

And then he was gone.

I woke up slowly the next morning, my mind lulled by the sounds of a constant steady rain and distant rolling thunder. The air in the house was fresh and cool, the tranquil drumming sound of raindrops pattering off the roof blanketed me like a warm, familiar quilt. I closed my eyes and consciously committed the moment to memory. I knew I was going to need it when I got back to California and my dad.

The last three days had been special for me. I guess you could say they were almost magical. While I hadn't understood what Mart was trying to say when he used that word to describe his friendship with David, I could now. It sounds odd to say I thought of the eighty-two year old man as the best friend I'd ever had, but that's exactly how I felt. Mart meant more to me at that moment than anyone else alive and I hated the idea of having to leave him.

The rain was going to slow my progress out in the yard but that was just fine by me. I knew better than to drag this out, I'd been forced to leave enough places and friends in my life to know that the longer I stayed, the harder it would be to say good by when it came time to move on, but I didn't have any control over the elements; that was God's territory and if he wanted to make it rain and keep me here an extra day, I wasn't going to bitch.

I'd stayed up late the night before, waiting for Mart to get home so I could talk to him some more but I ended up falling asleep before he got back. I never took my clothes off and the L'Amour book I'd been reading while I waited was lying on the floor where it had fallen sometime after I nodded off. I had a vague memory of hearing the old man rattling around out in the kitchen sometime during the night but it might have been a dream. I was going to have to get up and look out the window to see if Mart's old Ford was sitting out in the driveway to be sure he'd actually made it home...but not right now. For now I just wanted to lie on the couch and listen to the rain.

"Good day to sleep in, eh boy?"

My eyes popped open a little wider at the sound of Mart's voice but I didn't jump this time; I guess I was getting used to having Mart sitting in his chair every time I woke up on his couch. Propping myself up on one elbow, I turned and looked over at the old man.

"Don't you ever sleep in your bedroom?" I asked in mock exasperation.

Mart smiled a little as he lit a cigarette. While he still looked tired, that beaten look that had bothered me so much the night before was gone... or at least well hidden. Sitting up, I swung my legs off the couch and ran a hand through my hair. I glanced at the clock on the TV and saw it was just after eight.

"Wow, I guess I did sleep in," I said. Pulling a smoke from the pack in my pocket, I lit up my first cigarette of the day.

"I tried to wait up for you last night," I said, slipping my matches back into my pocket.

"Oh?" Mart said.

"Yeah," I said, looking at the floor. "I never got a chance to apologize to you for the way I acted yesterday after I-" I hesitated. I was going to say, 'after I figured out you wanted to die,' but I hated to even put the thought into words. While Mart was apparently ready to die, I wasn't ready to accept it and my saying it out loud seemed to be the equivalent of saying I was.

"...after I stormed out of here. I was rude to you and you didn't deserve that. I'm sorry," I finished.

Mart was silent. I glanced over and saw he was looking at me, his face a blank slate, telling nothing. I'd never had any trouble gauging the mood or attitude of any adult before but reading Mart was like trying to make sense out of a book written in Braille.

"Let's go for a ride, son." Mart snuffed his cigarette out in the ashtray and stood up. I gave him a puzzled look.

"C'mon," he prodded. "We skipped a stop on the fifty cent tour the other day. Let's go take a look."

Shrugging my shoulders, I stood up.

"Okay," I said.

The rain was already beginning to slack off as we walked out to the truck and I noticed the sky was clearing up on the horizon. Mart had grabbed an umbrella hanging from a nail in the mudroom as we left but it didn't look like we were going to need it. I thought about begging off on seeing the sight Mart wanted to show me so I could get to work on the yard as soon the rain stopped, but decided against it. The old man hadn't asked anything of me before now and I owed him. We climbed into the pick up and took off in the direction of Trufant.

The wet road was deserted. Light rain bounced off the roof of the old truck as the windshield wipers swished back and forth in time to a scratchy sounding Glen Campbell singing about what he'd do with a subway token and a dollar tucked inside his shoe. I stared out my window, looking at the now familiar sight of passing fields and trees through the rainwater rivulets snaking across the glass and daydreamed about how I might convince my dad to move out of the city and into the country. It was a childish, impossible thing to dream about, dad could never survive on the limited number of people waiting to be fleeced outside the city limits, but who could tell? Maybe it wasn't too late for my dad to change.

True to his nature, Mart turned on the first gravel road we came to and I quickly lost all sense of direction as we slowly meandered down muddy, rutted lanes. I just sat back in my seat and drank it all in... I didn't care if I ever saw another freeway, streetlight, or even the big yellow arches of a McDonalds again for as long as I lived. I loved the vast isolation of the countryside; the scattered bunches of trees, the pine stump fences, the patchwork fields, the sturdy looking farms with their massive barns, towering silos, and giant Tonka toy-like tractors and plows. Knowing I was going to have to leave all of these things behind in the next couple days only made watching them pass all the more exquisite and precious. Even before we reached our destination I had already decided to ask Mart if we could take a longer way home, the yard with its waiting dead weeds be damned.

Mart made another turn but didn't accelerate.

"It just occurred to me to ask you this, son," he said as the truck slowed going up a gentle grade. "How do you feel about cemeteries?"

Something deep down in my subconscious (*where are the headstones?*) squirmed a little at the word cemetery but I just ignored it out of hand. It seemed one thing or another was always doing some squirming around down there just lately.

"I don't mind them," I shrugged. "I used to live a couple blocks from one and I'd go there to read sometimes. Why?"

Mart nodded up ahead as he downshifted and fed a little gas to the motor. I looked up the slight grade in the road and saw a weather beaten picket fence guarding a wide empty block cut out of the woods on my side of the road.

"That's where we're headed," he said. "I know the idea of visiting a cemetery gives some folks the willies is why

I asked, but as long as it's all right with you..."

Mart looked at me and waited, giving me a chance to change my mind.

"Fine by me," I said.

Mart slowed the truck as we approached the lone two-track which led into the cemetery. An ancient granite archway spanned the gap in the picket fence; the words Sand Lake Cemetery etched in deeply chiseled letters across its face. Maneuvering the truck through the opening and into the cemetery, Mart parked off to one side of the two-track and shut down the engine. I started to reach for my door handle but stopped as I noticed Mart wasn't making any move to get out. I watched and waited as he rolled down his window and gazed reverently at the monuments around us. The rain had dropped off to almost nothing, the utter silence of the graveyard broken only by the occasional drop falling from the truck or nearby tree. It may have been the quietest place I'd ever been in my life.

The cemetery sat on the side of a hill, surrounded on all three sides by towering pines and oaks. The two-track ran up the center, dividing the numerous rows of settled headstones into two equal halves before splitting in two and circling around the border of the two halves to meet at the entrance where we were setting in the truck. It was a tiny place compared to those I was accustomed to seeing in the city. The cemeteries there almost always took up at least a full city block and some of them took up a lot more than that. The one I'd told Mart about where I'd go to read, that one ran nine blocks long and was two blocks wide. There had to have been at least thirty or forty thousand people buried there, maybe more; I doubted whether there could have been more than four or five hundred here. Over on the other side of the two-track I saw a headstone setting near the end of a row just beyond the hood of the truck. Leaning forward a little, I could read the name O'Mally inscribed in block script above a man and woman's name that had died back in the fifties. I looked over at Mart; hadn't he mentioned someone by that name once?

"You didn't know all the people buried here, did you?" I asked.

"Oh no," Mart said, shaking his head with a little smile. "This here's about the oldest cemetery in the whole county, son; I might be old but I'm not that old. From what I've been told there used to be a Baptist Church over here on the left side of the drive and the cemetery was over there on the right. Judging by the dates on the headstones I guess it took about a hundred years or so before the graveyard filled up, but by then the Baptists were ready to move on to a bigger building a little closer to town anyway so they tore the church down, doubled the size of the cemetery, and started in on this side. I recognize most all of the surnames of the folks buried in the older half, and I've some relation buried over there too. My dad's folks are over there, along with an aunt and uncle I never met but all those except for a few in the front two rows died long before I was even born. If I were to guess, I'd say it'd be a fair estimate to say I knew, or was at least acquainted, with probably a little more than half of the folks you see buried here."

I looked around in amazement at the headstones that surrounded us. Even at half, Mart was talking about roughly two hundred people! I didn't even know that many people by name! What must that feel like, outliving that many friends and relatives? Would you feel lucky? Like you'd won some kind of competition or something?

Every friend and neighbor I ever had is dead and buried and waiting for me up to the Sand Lake Cemetery and I'd like nothing more than to join them...

Mart's words floated back and I suddenly realized why we were here. The old man had brought me out here so I could see for myself why he was ready to die.

"Well I guess we won't be needing the umbrella after all," Mart said, glancing over at me. "Let's take a walk, son."

We climbed out of the truck and started up the little road. We took our time, the place almost seemed to demand it, and the day grew brighter as we walked. A light breeze picked up, rustling the leaves of the few trees and lilac bushes that grew amongst the graves, and now that the rain had stopped, the woods bordering the cemetery began to stir with squirrels and birds. A chipmunk stood up on his haunches as we approached his territory and scolded us for our intrusion before chattering a cheeky alarm and dashing away to the safety of his home beneath a black-speckled alabaster tablet. Incredibly intricate spider webs, still wet from the rain, glistened and dripped as bees and grasshoppers flew and jumped ahead of us, leading the way deeper into the cemetery. I never realized a place could be so busy and so peaceful at the same time.

The old man stopped to pick up an empty plastic flowerpot lying in the half moon of the track he was walking in and dropped it into a rusty, dented fifty-gallon drum as we passed. We walked on without talking, passing two or three more rows of headstones before Mart angled off the two-track to the left and started down a small, beaten path worn between two of the rows. As I fell in behind him I saw the path ended at a bench facing a neatly trimmed grave near the end of the row. A small bed of wildflowers stood in the shadow of the grave's headstone, a headstone that was shinier and newer than the others that surrounded it, and I knew that this was the grave of Mart's wife. The path we were following was his, worn there over time by his countless trips out to be with her. This was where the old man came to mourn.

The unbidden image of my mother's casket setting atop her open grave suddenly boiled up from my subconscious and I was helpless to stop it. Even though I had only been there once, I knew without a doubt there were no paths leading to my mom's grave.

Oh, why did you have to bring me here, I wondered.

My mom was buried in a flat, colorless cemetery that didn't allow headstones or flowers or anything else that might impede the groundskeepers from mowing the grass in the minimum amount of time. I-75, one of the busiest six lane freeways in the United States, ran just beyond the fence next to her grave, so close you could feel the ground rumblings of passing semis through the soles of your shoes. The only funeral she was given was a graveside service attended by five people (seven, if you wanted to count the two cemetery employees watching from the truck who had brought the backhoe they'd used to dig her grave, and would use again to cover her casket as soon as we left); her parents, their priest or minister or whatever you wanted to call the man that taught them to banish their daughter for not believing as they did, a social services woman from the city of Detroit, a huge, stupid woman who had gotten lost while driving me there in her city issued blue Pinto, and me. The service was short and sweet and tailored specifically for the supposedly grieving parents of the black sheep so tragically taken before realizing the woes of living outside the flock of the true believers. My grandmother cried during the service but my grandfather didn't and neither did I... not until after the sham priest led his followers away from me. They had tried to talk to me- my grandparents and their priest. They tried telling me how sorry they were, not for turning their only daughter away when she needed them, but for God's decision to take her away rather than allowing her to live a miserable life in sin, and they asked if I wanted to come stay with them. They didn't mention how long I could stay, nor did they make any mention of my having to repent from my evil ways of the world and join them in their beliefs as a condition of my staying, but I knew. I knew and I hated them for it. They didn't give a damn about me; they were just looking for the window dressing my conversion would bring to adorn their all knowing and perfect souls in the eyes of their God. I told them all to kiss my ass and go to hell and the priest, after giving me a sorrowful yet somehow pious look, shook his head at me and led them away. The social services lady tried to put her arm around me but I shrugged her off and walked up to my mom's satin pink casket to say my goodbye alone. I cried then.

I was crying now.

"You all right, son?"

I looked up and saw Mart standing in front of me an instant before I would have run into him. I stopped and looked away, quickly wiping at the tears running down my face. I felt Mart's hand on my shoulder.

"There's nothing wrong with crying, son," he said. "It's the not crying that'll get you."

That was it; I lost it. The wall I'd so carefully built and tended over the last year crumbled and gave way and everything came pouring out. Mart put an arm around my shoulders. I turned and buried my face against his chest and cried. I cried for my mom, I cried for Cindy, I cried for Mart, I cried for myself. I was no longer a child, I knew now what I needed to know to go on alone, but the knowledge hadn't come cheap. The protective scales of youth had fallen from my eyes and I could see all the irretrievable things that had been lost, the love, the happiness, the companionship, the endless childhood days in the sun. I could appreciate now how important these things were. Knowing they were gone just tore me up.

The storm eventually passed and, suddenly self-conscious, I stepped away from Mart. Reaching into his pocket, he handed me his handkerchief and gave me a pat on the shoulder as he turned and began tending to the flowers growing on his wife's grave. I sat down on the bench and got myself cleaned up.

"Sorry about that," I said when Mart finally stood up again. The old man gave me a 'don't be stupid' look and eased himself down on the bench next to me. As he moved out of the way I was able to read the headstone in front of us for the first time. It said:

ASH

I shall go to her

For she cannot return to me

Mary Elisabeth	*Martin Jonas*
1893 - 1971	**1892 -**

Fresh tears sprang up in my eyes as I read the epitaph Mart had chosen. With my emotions still churning away so dangerously close to the surface, I had to look away.

The next headstone over, a smaller and much older looking stone, belonged to Joan Elaine Ash, born 1913, died 1918, and to the right of that stood an identical marker with the name August Jacob Ash, 1914 to 1918; the son and daughter that had died in the flu epidemic. While I had never doubted Mart's story for an instant, seeing the graves of his children made them real for me, almost tangible, and I felt a pang of remorse that they had died so young.

From where I was sitting on the bench I counted at least thirty gravestones engraved with the name Ash. Seven of them belonged to Mart and Mary Ash's children, the year of their deaths all predated their mother's by at least twenty years. The remainder belonged to other members of Mart's family, his parents, his brothers (three with wives and children, two without), and two of his sisters that had died too young to marry. A wave of pity for the old man washed over me and, while I still abhorred the idea of Mart wanting to die, I caught the barest glimpse of understanding why he was ready to go.

"I've always liked cemeteries."

I looked at Mart, totally baffled by his quiet statement.

"Mary and I used to pass a lot of Sunday afternoons visiting graveyards just like this one," he said, his eyes slipping slowly over the tombstones around us. "Most times there'd be a grave of a friend or relative to visit but not always. Sometimes we wouldn't know a single person but we'd stop in anyway, just to take a stroll and enjoy the peace and quiet." Slipping a cigarette between his lips, Mart glanced at me as he lit up.

"I guess it might sound kind of odd to some, our walking amongst the dead, reading headstones and pondering the misfortune and loss of folks we'd never known, but we'd had our share of losses too; we'd shed enough tears over our own to know these places aren't here for the dead. They're here to remind the living that the dead buried beneath these stones once lived and loved and laughed and cried just like everybody else."

The old man paused, looking at the graves of his wife and children. Behind us the sun broke free of the clouds and flooded the cemetery.

"Most folks buried in older places like this don't have anyone left to remember who they were," he lamented. "Their people have all moved or died or just plain forgotten about their Uncle Jim or the nice lady who used to bake pies for the church social, and it's almost like they never existed at all. The only thing that keeps most of these folks out here from fading away altogether is old farts like me... and maybe the occasional couple that happens along on a Sunday afternoon to pause a moment and wonder what kind of life might have been lived between the dates on these stones."

I didn't get it. Mart was talking like he thought the people buried around us were still here, just hanging out, waiting for visitors.

"But I thought you believed in God," I said. "Don't

you think these people are already in heaven... or hell?"

"Yes I do," Mart nodded patiently. "I believe every one of these folks met their just reward the very second they took their last breath; that's what I meant when I said these places aren't here for the dead. I'm not talking about their souls, son, I'm talking about the memories they left behind. You're too young to have given it any thought yet, but as you get older I think you'll find that being dead and being forgotten are two completely different things. God might be the one to decide how long each one of us gets to walk this earth but it's up to us to decide how we want to be remembered."

I couldn't understand what Mart was saying, and frankly, I didn't care. I had just about had my fill of death and memories and looking at gravestones. Walking away from Mart was going to be hard enough as it was, I knew all this stuff was going to come back to haunt me when that time arrived.

"You didn't have to bring me out here, you know."

"What's that, son?" Mart gave me a puzzled look.

"I know you want to die," I said miserably, avoiding his eyes, "you didn't have to bring me out here to show me why. I don't think it's right and I wish I knew how to change your mind but I don't think that's ever going to happen, so it's better if I just go as soon as I finish up the yard. You've done enough for me; you've kept your promise and I'll never forget the things you told me. You don't have to worry about me."

Mart chewed on that for a minute before replying.

"Well, I hate to disappoint you, Skippy," he said, taking one last drag off his cigarette, "but that's not the reason you and I are sitting here today."

Leaning over, the old man reached down under the bench and came up with an old Folgers coffee can. Peeling back the plastic lid, he dropped his still smoldering cigarette butt inside before pressing the lid back down and returning the can back under the bench. Sitting up, he pulled a lined piece of notebook paper from his breast pocket. The paper was neatly folded but deeply creased and wrinkled, as if it had been picked out of the garbage after being wadded up and thrown away.

"This is why we're here," he said, unfolding the paper and holding it out to me. "Somebody stuck this under my windshield wiper while I was having a beer up to Charlie's last night."

I took the paper from Mart's fingers and read:

Free to good home

Older mixed breed dog

Family pet - Good with Kids

Moving to apartment that

doesn't allow pets 8/01/74

121 Maple Street, Trufant

I looked at Mart, not sure what to say. Mart stared back at me, shaking his head.

"I was pretty damned disgusted with you when I first saw that." The old man nodded at the flyer I was holding. I opened my mouth to protest but stopped as he held up a hand.

"I didn't know how you pulled it off," he said with an ironic smile, "how you managed to write that up, get it down to the bar and put it on my truck during the half hour I'd been gone, but I knew it was you that had done it, I knew it just as sure as I'm sitting here right now. It had to have been you, it was just too... what was the word you used the other day? Convenient! It was just too convenient, finding something like that on my truck barely twelve hours after you asked me about taking in a dog. I wadded it up, tossed it into the bed of the truck and decided right then and there that you and I were going to come to a meeting of the minds when I got home. Who were you to try and tell me I didn't have the right to want to die, anyway? My God, you're just a kid! Oh, you and I were going to have a talk all right, and I was going to set you straight... but then as I opened the door to get into my truck, I saw there was another flyer just like this one under the windshield wiper of the Chevy sitting next to me. I looked around a little more and saw another one on the next car and the next... every car in the lot had one of these flyers, not just mine. I couldn't move. I just stood there, looking at all those papers flopping in the wind, waving at me like a bunch of school kids trying to catch my attention, and I got scared.

"I started off by telling myself I was being silly, that it was just some kind of weird coincidence, finding a paper like that on my truck, but I had some trouble getting that horse to run. I finally had to admit to myself that I knew how that flyer had come to be there and I knew why."

Mart paused, gazing at his wife's gravestone.

"And it wouldn't surprise me at all to find my wife had a hand in it too." The old man smiled fondly at the thought but the mood was fleeting, the smile faded as quickly as it had appeared.

"Mary was everything to me, son," he said quietly. "The one true love of my life. She was half of me and I was half of her and losing her was like losing my eyes or my legs, I was crippled and I knew I'd never be whole until we were together again. Without Mary here, right or wrong didn't apply to me any more, the game was over, the daylight was gone and God had called olli, olli, ox in free. The very fact that I was still here to draw another breath without her was wrong, the thought of ever allowing myself to hope for anything more would have been an unpardonable sin against her memory and I wouldn't allow it. I gave up my right to care whether or not tomorrow ever came the day she died and I started waiting for God to take me home. I'd done all the living I cared to do and if God didn't want to cooperate, well, I'd just wait him out. I guess the idea that I might come to regret all those wasted waiting days was always lurking around somewhere in the back of my mind but I didn't really give it much thought; I knew any regrets I had were going to die right along with me when I went and there wasn't a soul left on this earth to care how I spent my days in the meantime. There wasn't anyone left to remember..."

The old man turned and looked at me.

"You remember that first night when you came back after you got your fur up and took off? You were headed up to the house to get some sleep when you stopped and asked me why it was that I had bought food and laid out the bedding on the couch for you after you left; you remember what I told you?"

"Sure," I said, thinking back. "You said you weren't expecting me to come back but you were hoping that I would."

"I was hoping you would," Mart repeated. "That was the first time since the day Mary died that I had hoped for anything other than my last breath. I wouldn't admit it to myself right then, of course, but that's when I had to start wondering just exactly how crippled up I really was. How can a man want to die when he still has hope?"

Mart leaned over, took the flyer from my hand and folded it back up.

"I'm too old to be making any promises here, Ken Malone," he said, looking me in the eye. "You can stay or go as you please, you say you're okay now and I believe that you are, I'll not stand in your way, but I want you to know that I'd truly hate to see you leave here knowing your memory of me, the memory you'll carry with you till the day you die, will be a memory of the man that I was before I met you."

I dropped my eyes and looked away, not knowing what to say. I knew what I wanted to say... I desperately wanted to believe the old man had changed, I wanted to say Yeah, sure, I'll stick around for a while, but I couldn't... I couldn't because I was afraid. Sure, Mart felt different right now, but what about tomorrow, or the next day? What about next week? How would I feel if I stayed even for a few extra days and he decided to give up on life again? So the old man was taking the pledge, big deal. I must have heard my dad swear a hundred times that he was never going to touch another drop of booze for as long as he lived but he had always gone right back to it. I started off believing him at first but after the fiftieth time or so I began to understand that dad probably wasn't going to stop, at least not this time. Then toward the end I'd just roll my eyes and tell myself to expect to smell booze on his breath by five that afternoon- and, in that respect at least, Dad had never let me down once. But in spite of everything I did to guard against getting my hopes up and expecting too much, that first promise-breaking whiff of alcohol still hurt me, every single time. I guess I always wanted to believe my dad would some day keep his word. I always held onto a secret hope...

(*How can a man want to die when he still has hope?*)

My spirits lifted as a seed sprouted in my mind and quickly grew to towering heights.

I turned and looked at Mart, suddenly understanding what it was that we'd both come so dangerously close to giving up- what it was that neither of us could find within ourselves yet had somehow found a way to give to each other- and I understood why I had to stay, at least for a while.

We gave each other hope.

"I suppose I could stick around a little while longer," I said, trying to keep a smile off my face and failing miserably. "Got any more chores around the house you need doing?"

"Well," Mart considered, scratching his chin thoughtfully. "I am going to be needing somebody to pick up dog poop. You interested?"

"I'm your man," I laughed.

"All right then," Mart said, slapping his thighs and standing up. "What do you say we go pick up my new dog and head for home?"

"Okay," I said.

And that's exactly what we did.

The dog Mart adopted that day was a black lab/German shepherd mix named Molly. The woman that gave her to us, a middle aged, divorced mother with two girls, had gotten Molly as a puppy just after her divorce and she told us she'd been worried sick she was going to end up taking the old dog to the pound when it came time for her to move. She told us she'd written up at least fifty of those flyers the day before and then her and her daughters had driven around and put one up in every store and gas station they could find in Trufant, Greenville, and Coral, but they still had twelve left over when they were done. The woman told us they were driving past Charlie's Bar on their way back home when she stopped on a whim and had her girls stick one on each of the cars in the parking lot, just to keep from throwing them away. A perfectly plausible, reasonable explanation for how a flier advertising a free dog found its way under Mart's windshield wiper... until you stop and think about it for a minute. How many random strands of individual lives had to intersect at the precise angle, at the precise tension, the precise time and length and mood, to bring three totally unrelated beings together at the exact moment they all needed each other the most?

God works in mysterious ways?

The moon is in the seventh house?

A thousand monkeys tapping away on a thousand typewriters?

God, fate, or coincidence, everyone faces the riddle eventually and, whether you know it or not, everyone makes a decision. While we are all afforded the opportunity to recognize that the decision is ours to make, few take advantage of it… most just end up living out their entire lives without even realizing they've made a choice.

Molly missed her family for a while but, like me, she'd never lived in the country before and she took right to it. The poor old girl had never had much of an opportunity to be a dog before then; other than the occasional walk on the end of a leash, she'd lived her whole life in the cramped, smelly little pen we found her in the day we picked her up. Like a lot of city dogs, she'd been relegated to spend the first eight years of her existence trapped inside a six by six foot chain link cage, forced to watch as the world lived on without her.

"Nice enough woman, I guess," Mart said as we drove away with Molly sitting up on the bench seat between us, "but there are more than a few people in this world that have no business owning a pet and that's one of them."

Now eight years old is getting up there when you're talking about a good size dog like Molly, she had to weigh ninety pounds, easy, but you'd never have known she was that old to watch her romp around out in the yard. Living in the country brought out the puppy in her, anything that flew, ran or smelled was interesting; every leaf blowing across the yard had to be investigated, every scent in the wind had to be savored, tracked down, and- if the source could be located- rolled in, any creature found within the confines of the yard had to be chased until they exited said yard, and any existing hole in the ground- whether it be in the yard, the field, or muddy ditch- had to be dug deeper and wider and as quickly and frantically as possible. Every day was a celebration for Molly and she took advantage of every minute of every day she had.

The old man was right; you can learn a lot from a dog.

Molly died in her sleep at the foot of Mart's chair in the fall of '77. Mart and I buried her out in the yard next to Mindy and I guess we both cried a little.

Cindy and I got to know each other a little better over the next couple of years but we were never really close. Oh, we were friends. I used to ride my bicycle down to the bar some mornings and we'd talk while I helped her get the place ready to open up for the day, and if the place wasn't too busy on the days Mart and I drove up to the bar for dinner, Cindy would come out and sit with us and talk for a while- but we never really had much of a relationship. We were brother and sister, nothing could ever change that, and I know we loved each other, but Cindy's childhood wounds had never had a chance to heal as mine would. No one had ever stepped up to help her out back when she still had a chance at being whole... or if someone did, Cindy had already been too far gone to take the chance. Our conversations were always neutral and cautious and, while Cindy always took a vicarious interest in hearing about the things happening in my life, she was never interested in talking about hers. Her life was far from perfect, she knew it, I knew it, probably half the town knew it, but her problems were her own and they weren't open for discussion. She accepted the hand life had dealt her and she played it out the only way she knew how.

Neither of us ever saw our dad again. We both tried to get in touch with him off and on over the next year or so but we never had any luck. Cindy called and left messages with the woman who had given her dad's phone number in the first place, an elderly aunt of my dad's who I never even knew existed until Cindy told me about her, while I ran up what must have been some pretty hefty toll calls on Mart's phone, calling the different bars and party stores I knew my dad would frequent if he were still living in Venice. A couple of the people I talked to told me they knew who Leo Malone was and yes, he was still around, he'd just been in a day or two before and sure, they'd give him the number I left just as soon as they saw him again... but he never called me back. Maybe my dad never went back to those particular bars, maybe he and Sheila had moved on to greener pastures in Los Angeles or San Francisco. Or maybe he did stop in to those bars, only the people I had talked to weren't working that night, or if they were, maybe they didn't see him or maybe they were mad at him, maybe they'd lost the phone number or maybe they never even wrote it down in the first place. I must have come up with twenty different scenarios to explain why my father never called me back that year and I desperately wanted to believe one of them was true. I guess I still do. While he might not have been much of a father to me when I needed him, he was still my dad and I always loved him, I would have given him another chance if only he had called.

I never did ask for the other half of Mart's hundred-dollar bill. He offered it to me several times over the four years I lived with him but I wouldn't take it. He always looked a little disgusted with me when I turned him down, especially after I got my license and started driving that old Ford Galaxie that had been stored out in the barn (even with the money I earned stocking shelves and bagging groceries down to DeWalls Foodmart, I did a lot of walking and bumming rides while my car sat in the driveway waiting for a part I couldn't afford to buy until payday) but he never once asked me *why* I wouldn't take the other half. Looking back now I think he had an inkling of how I felt, I think he may have suspected I looked at the two halves of that bill as a kind of talisman, a talisman that could only work to keep the two of us together as long as the two halves were kept apart... but like I said, he never asked.

Mart died on December 22, 1978, seven years to the day after he lost his wife.

I had just finished my first semester of college at Ferris State, a reputable public school less than a two-hour drive from Trufant. While I had chosen Ferris because it was close enough to allow me to come home on the weekends to stay with Mart, I hadn't been home since the beginning of October.

I was going to school on a full academic scholarship compliments of the State of Michigan and one of the requirements of keeping my ride was I had to maintain a 2.75 grade point average. Like ninety percent of all freshman in college, I wasn't sure yet what I wanted to be when I grew up but since I had to put down something on the application, I had listed a split major; electrical engineering with a minor in education. A degree in electrical engineering requires a lot of math and, to make a long story short, I got a little cocky and chose to ignore the school counselor's recommendation that I take Algebra 2, a prep class which wouldn't count towards my major, and instead enrolled myself in Calculus 1. The counselor, a tired looking, older woman of about fifty who had apparently grown accustomed to being ignored by snotty little freshman, just shrugged and shook her head as she watched me fill out the form.

"It's your funeral," she said as she signed the bottom of the form and handed it back to me. Confident in my abilities, I flashed her an undaunted smile and took my enrollment sheet to the registrar's office.

I strolled into my first Calculus class with my ten-pound copy of Calculus- An Introduction under my arm, a single sheet of notebook paper in my breast pocket guarding against the unlikely event I had to take a note or two, and a paperback novel in my back pocket for when I got bored. Fifty axiom, theorem, and tangent filled minutes later, I walked out of the classroom confident only in my knowledge that I was by far the stupidest person in the class. The smart thing to do would have been to drop the class and take Algebra 2 but that would have required a visit to the same counselor who had tried to advise me to do that in the first place and I couldn't bring myself to do that. For the next three months my life revolved around Calculus workshops and study groups, a copy of Algebra 2 I had bought off one of my roommates after he dropped out of school, meals of Snickers bars and Cokes out of the dorm's vending machines, and very little sleep. I started the semester driving home every weekend and studying up in my room until it was time to go back on Sunday but after a month or so of seeing me just long enough to say hello and goodbye, Mart had seen enough.

"Here," he said, handing me three rolls of dimes as he walked me out to my car one Sunday night. The sun had just settled below the horizon and the calm peaceful air around us felt crisp and melancholy; summer was gone for the year and winter was just days away. Seeing what Mart had given me, I stopped and gave the old man a confused look.

"Next time you want to see if I'm still kicking you just give me a call," he said.

"But-" I started to protest.

"I don't need any buts, Skippy," he growled as he slipped a cigarette into his mouth. "I guess I'm old enough to look after myself. You just stay up there to school and concentrate on your studies or you and I are going to go to knuckle junction, you hear?"

The old man paused as he lit his cigarette.

"And besides," he said with a hint of a smile as he snapped the Zippo closed, "how am I suppose to entertain my lady friends on the weekends with you around, did you ever ask yourself that?"

While I didn't like the idea of not coming home to check on Mart, I couldn't help but smile a little at his crack about his lady friends. Mart and I both knew there weren't any other ladies in his life. Oh, he'd kept busy over the last four years, fishing down to the lake and working around the house and answering questions a couple afternoons a week over to the Kent County Historical Society Museum in Cedar Springs, but he had always had a hard and fast rule of not accepting any of the frequent dinner invitations he received from the many widows who offered them. Knowing what I did about the old man, I can't say as I ever blamed him.

"All right," I relented. While Mart talked a good fight I knew he was only half serious, I could come back anytime I wanted and I knew he'd be happy to see me... but I also knew he was right. Thanks to my stubbornness, I was seriously worried that I might end up losing my scholarship and the thought of failing so early on in my life scared the hell out of me, I needed every hour of study time I could get.

The two of us started toward my car again but now that we both knew I probably wouldn't be coming back for a couple months, we took our time getting there. Reaching the car, I set my books and my three rolls of dimes on the hood, turned and leaned back against the car. Mart sidled up and joined me and we both sat there, silently looking at the only place I would ever think of as home.

Mart and I had accomplished a lot in the four years we'd had together; we'd trimmed the lower branches of the two pine trees, painted and re-roofed the house (quite an accomplishment for me as I was deathly afraid of heights), burned the remnants of the old chicken coop, reseeded the lawn, started a vegetable garden that seemed to get bigger with every spring, hauled away the rusted farm implements from around the barn, built a tool shed in the backyard... the list just went on and on. The old place looked warm and inviting now, and everywhere I looked I saw memories of the two of us working together, talking and laughing.

"God, I love it here," I whispered as the soft yet never silent voice of the motionless fields sighed around us.

"I know you do, son," Mart nodded quietly. "But you'll never be able to feel the same way about this place if you come back here without finishing what you've set out to do. Maybe you'll pass that class you got yourself into and maybe you won't; the important thing for you to do is to keep your chin up and give 'er everything you've got... there's no shame in failing as long as you try."

The old man paused and we both looked up to

watch a low flying V formation of honking Canadian Geese pass by as they headed south.

"Your momma's watching over you, boy," Mart went on after they'd gone, "and it wouldn't surprise me none but if Mary weren't sitting right there next to her, cheering you on as if you were her own. You go on back to school now and make 'em proud. Win, lose, or draw, I'll still be here when you get back, I'll promise you that."

I looked over to Mart and gave him a half-hearted smile.

"Oh, thanks," I moaned. "Like I didn't have enough pressure, you had to go and drag my mom into this."

Mart smiled as he reached out and gave me a hug.

"Go on now, son," he said, patting me on the back. "I'll see you when I see you."

"I'll be calling you," I said as we stepped apart.

"I'll be here," Mart said, already turning to walk back toward the house. I watched him go until he rounded the corner and then, after taking one last, long look around the place, I climbed into my car and drove away.

Two months later I remembered the things Mart had said that day as I drove home from school.

My semester had officially ended at three thirty-five that day after I handed in my calculus exam. Thanks to my decent grades in my other four classes (two A's and two B's) I knew I had my G.P.A. in the bag even before I took the test, the only question left had been whether or not I could score well enough on the calculus exam to bring the D plus average I had going in the class up to a C or better. Anything over a C plus on the exam would bring my class average up to a solid C and my semester in hell would count toward my major; anything less meant I'd have to take the course over again. While everyone in his class knew that Dr. Doctor (no kidding, that was his name), the skinny, anal-retentive, hairless little man that taught the course, checked and graded all exams immediately after they were handed in, all the other deadwood in the class had dropped out after the first day- leaving me alone with twenty-one human calculators- and I was the only one waiting for him out in the hall when he came out at three forty-five.

"Excuse me, Dr-" I started.

"B minus," he sniffed with a pained expression as he minced by without missing a step.

I couldn't believe it. I stared after the little guy in shocked wonder as he walked down the hall. I had made it.

"THANK YOU," I yelled politely to the prof just as the door at the far end of the corridor closed behind him. Feeling lighter than air, I laughed out loud as I turned and ran down the stairwell behind me. Five minutes later I was in my car and heading out.

While we were in the grips of a typical snowy Michigan winter, a rare sunny December day reflected my mood as I drove away from school towards home. It was incredibly cold, ten degrees above zero according to the d.j. on the radio, and tiny crystalline slivers of snow twinkled as they floated down to dust the ground, but my car was warm, the roads were dry, and WLAV, the AOR station out of Grand Rapids, was coming in just as clear as a bell. The crushing weight of pending doom had been lifted from my shoulders and I felt like a vindicated man who had just been released from a dark, dank prison, I was as free as a bird and I was headed home.

Days are short in Michigan during the winter and by the time I rolled into Stanwood, a tiny little village thirty-five miles or so outside of Big Rapids, the sun had slipped down behind a dark, angry looking cloudbank that was swooping in out of the west and my mood had grown decidedly pensive. It was snowing harder now; the wind was picking up considerably and the roads were getting more treacherous by the mile.

It took me twenty minutes to cover the ten miles that separates Stanwood from its twin tiny town of Morley and, other than an occasional heart stopping stretch or two of not being able to see the Ford Emblem perched out on the lip of my hood, visibility through the wind driven bullets of snow had deteriorated down to a fairly steady 50 feet. Knowing Mart would be worried when I didn't show up by six (I'd called him the night before and told him when to expect me) I pulled into the only gas station in town to give the old man a call.

"Your lucky day," I heard as I stomped the snow off my shoes after walking inside. I looked up and saw a heavyset man with a magazine in his hand perched on a stool behind the counter.

"Two minutes later and you'd have been shit outa luck, guy," he said, tossing the magazine down next to the cash register.

"You close at six?" I asked, looking up at the emblazoned STP clock on the wall behind him.

"I do tonight," he said, pushing himself up off the stool. "Just got off the phone with my wife. According to the TV the State Police are telling folks to stay off the roads. Where you headed?"

"Trufant," I said, looking around the station for a phone.

"Is that right," the man said skeptically. "What can I get for you?"

"Pack of Marlboro reds," I answered distractedly. "You got a payphone here?"

"Nope," the man said, tossing the smokes on the counter. "That'll be fifty-five cents." Pulling out my wallet, I handed him a dollar bill.

"Any chance I could make a call on your phone?" I asked as he rang up my purchase.

"Local call?" he asked, raising his eyebrows.

"No, but I'd be happy to pay you."

"Sorry," he said, handing me my change. "Last fella I let do that ended up calling down to Alabama. Gave me a dollar for a call that cost me three bucks."

I slipped my change into my pocket and looked around, trying to come up with a way to make my call.

"How about if I call collect?" I asked.

The man's expression didn't look promising.

"I just want to call home to let somebody know I'm running late," I added. "If I don't get hold of him I'm afraid he might come out in this crap looking for me."

The man considered my predicament for a second and finally shrugged.

"I guess that'd work," he nodded. Reaching back for the phone, he picked up the receiver, handed it to me and dialed zero. The operator came on and I gave her the number.

"Who shall I say is calling?" she asked. Just as I opened my mouth to give her my name, a thought occurred to me and I smiled.

"Skippy," I said. "Skippy Calculus Malone."

"One moment please," the humorless voice said. Still smiling at my own joke, I glanced up at the counterman. Giving me an impatient look, he turned and checked the clock. Suddenly feeling kind of stupid, I looked away and began counting the distant sounding rings of Mart's phone. I started getting worried after ring number five.

I had made it my habit to call Mart after dark because that was the one time of day I could always count on him answering. And he always- and I mean <u>always</u> answered by the fourth ring. By the time the operator spoke up again I had counted ten and was waiting on number eleven.

"I'm sorry sir, no one is answering."

"Could you let it ring a couple more times, operator?" I said, a cold finger of dread running down my spine. "I'm sure he's there."

"I'm sorry, sir," she said after another five rings.

"Would you care to try again later?"

I dropped the receiver on the counter and ran out of the gas station to my car.

Driving was a nightmare. I had seen quite a few snowstorms in the four years I'd been in Michigan but this one was far and away the worst. Keeping my car in the right lane wasn't even an option; most of the time I wasn't even sure where the road was!

My body was a tense coiled spring of apprehension; I drove hunched over the steering wheel, pushing the old car as fast as I dared (which is to say I was doing maybe 15 miles an hour, tops), praying I wouldn't come upon a slower vehicle or God forbid, a jackknifed semi. The cone formed by my headlights illuminated a white, never ending tunnel in front of me, a tunnel broken only by occasional tight dervishes of swirling snow screaming in from the west that would buffet the car back and forth to the limit of her four decidedly weak shocks as they broke through the walls and filled the tunnel with snow. Unwilling to take my straining eyes off the road for even a second I lit my cigarettes by sense of feel, using the lighter from the dashboard. I steered as if I were piloting a barge, I worked the gas and brake pedals as though they were made of glass, always fighting to keep the back wheels in line with the front. And through it all I never stopped thinking of Mart.

He was gone. I knew it even as my mind manufactured any number of reasons explaining why he hadn't been there to answer the phone. The scenarios ranged from the innocuous (he'd walked out to retrieve something from his truck, he'd been down in the basement relighting the furnace pilot after it had been blown out by a rogue gust of wind down the exhaust flue, he was sitting on the toilet) to the dire (he'd slipped and fell as he walked out to his truck, breaking his hip and was slowly freezing to death as his body disappeared under the driving snow) but they were just all so much tripe. I knew Mart was dead, I could feel it in my soul. He'd had a heart attack or a stroke and his body was lying on the floor where he had fallen, waiting for me.

It all fit; my euphoric mood hours earlier, my weekly perfunctory phone calls, Mart's promise that he'd be waiting for me when I got home- wasn't that exactly the way bad things happened, didn't tragedies always wait until you least expected them before coming up out of nowhere to blindside you? Hadn't things been going a little too well lately, a little too easy? A little too perfect?

I should have seen it coming. I should have known there'd be a price to pay for the miracle of the last four years that had been my life. I should have known and I should have taken steps to guard against it. I should have appreciated my pain free life more and I should have done more with it, I should have taken advantage of even the smallest opportunities offered and savored every one. I should have grabbed hold of every waking moment and reveled in the ride while it lasted.

I should have gotten out of bed and walked outside to look at the stars the night the whippoorwill took up roost outside my bedroom window and woke me up... but I didn't. I should have ridden into town with Mart when he asked me to that Saturday two years ago... but instead I'd stayed home to watch an old Andy Griffith rerun... a show I'd seen before and didn't even like! Oh, it was all so obvious now.

I'd brought this on myself. I had allowed myself to forget how much I'd gained and I had taken the gift of my carefree life for granted. I had taken Mart for granted. I'd somehow lost sight of my appreciation for all the things the old man had done for me and now he was gone.

I prayed. I prayed for just one more chance to see the old man, to talk with him and thank him- one more chance to tell him I loved him. I offered God an open-ended bargain; I'd give anything he asked in exchange for one last opportunity to erase the enormous weight of regret that was crushing my heart. I could see now all the moments I'd squandered, all I wanted was a chance to win one of them back. If it was Mart's time to go, that was fine, I knew he was ready. All I asked of God was that he not be taken until I saw him one last time. There were so many things I had to tell him, so many things I'd always taken for granted that he knew.

So many things I should have told him when I'd had the chance.

I had a little less than a mile to go to reach the house when I finally went off the road. It had been a good two hours since I left the gas station and while the snow was still falling with a vengeance, the wind had already played itself out. I probably would have made it all the way to the driveway had it not been for a Kent County snowplow appearing out of the falling snow in front of me as I crested a little knoll. The driver of the truck, apparently assuming there wasn't anyone stupid enough to be out driving a vehicle not equipped with tire chains and a plow, was running right down the middle of the lane. Cranking the wheel to get out of his way, my right tires slipped off the edge of the black top and the snow did the rest, sucking me off the road into the ditch. The car went from 20 miles an hour to stopped in less than ten feet.

I tried to open my door but the packed snow pressing against the front and sides of the car wouldn't allow it. Opening my window, I wriggled out and struggled through the snow out to the freshly plowed surface of the road. Ten minutes later I was standing at our mailbox.

I stopped to catch my breath, looking up at the house as I bent over to rest with my hands on my thighs. Everything looked normal; Mart's snow covered truck was sitting in the driveway right where it always was, the pool of light from the mercury vapor lamp we had put up in the back yard that summer was just visible through the huge fluffy flakes of falling snow, and there was a light burning in the kitchen. Everything looked normal... except for the living room. The living room was dark, but it wasn't quite dark enough. The TV and all the lamps were off, I could see that, but there was some kind of glow in the room, a hint of dancing pastel light that invoked in me a marshmallow feeling of happiness and well being ... and the scent of pine. My mind finally made the connection and I realized I was looking at the soft red and green hues of Christmas tree lights.

Mart had decorated the tree.

While hundreds of Christmas memories from the past flooded my mind, the memory of one special night glowed especially bright. I grabbed onto that memory and, as scared as I was at what I might find when I went inside the house, I suddenly felt a little better as I realized that no matter how things turned out in the next few minutes- even if my premonition were true and Mart was gone- I had found some redemption hidden among my regrets, a memory I could turn to for solace if the worst had already come to pass.

Molly and I found the young pine growing in the blurred line between woodlot and weeds out on the far edge of the north field. Six foot tall. Conical. Fairly symmetrical. It was perfect.

I cut it down two days later while Mart was in the house watching the Lions lose to the Packers. I dragged it home and hid it in the barn.

Mart's daily trips out to the cemetery were shorter now, whether because of the change of season or in his attitude, I didn't know, but I was never alone in the house for more than forty-five minutes a day. Since I wanted this to be a surprise, I allowed myself just thirty minutes after he left each day to get out to the barn and do what I could with the tree before running back to the house so I'd be there when he pulled back in. I worked on the tree for six days in a row. I snipped off irregular branches, made a stand, strung the lights, draped the tinsel. I did everything except hang the fragile glass ornaments; I'd do that after I carried the tree inside the house.

Mart never suspected a thing.

The tree was ready to go three days before Christmas... and we got snowed in. It snowed nonstop for the next two days and while Mart could have easily gotten his truck out of the driveway (I must have shoveled it twenty times or more to keep it clear those two days), the county snowplows were concentrating on the main roads and ours wasn't one of them. Our road, along with all the other roads within ten miles of Trufant, was impassible.

The plows finally came by around two in the afternoon on Christmas Eve. Being old and patient, Mart gave them a couple of hours to clear the rest of the roads he'd have to take to get to the cemetery before finally leaving about five. I was running out to the barn before he hit second gear on his way out.

I managed to wrestle the tree about ten feet away from the barn door before admitting the obvious; I wasn't going to be able to get the tree up to the house, the snow was nearly up to my waist and the partially decorated tree was too heavy to carry above my head. I was screwed. I was going to have to wait until Mart got back and he was going to have to help me carry the tree up to the house and my Christmas present to him would be tarnished. Unless...

I ran back into the barn, stripped the tarp off the old car, and ran back to the tree. I laid the tree down on the tarp and started pulling. It worked! I had the tree inside the house in under five minutes.

Not wanting Mart to see the tree from the driveway

as he drove up, I was hanging the last few ornaments by the dim light of a dying flashlight when I saw the flash of his headlights splash across the wall. Praying the old strings of bulbous lights would work when I plugged them in (there wasn't any electricity out in the barn and in my rush to get everything else done after getting the tree into the house I had never thought to test them) I ran out to the kitchen and unscrewed the light bulb hanging in the fixture above the table. I wanted the house completely dark when I plugged in the tree for Mart. That done, I ran back into the living room, hunkered down next to the couch and waited there with the plug to the Christmas tree lights poised at the wall outlet.

I heard the squeak of the screen door opening followed by the meatier sound of the inner wooden door as it swung in. I listened as Mart stomped the snow off his boots, my heart pounding in my chest. While I was excited at the prospect of surprising Mart with the tree, I was a little worried too; in spite of all we'd been through in the last few months, the two of us were still getting to know each other and I wasn't a hundred percent sure I was doing the right thing.

"Well shit," I heard Mart mutter mildly as he tried the light switch.

"In here," I called.

I aimed the flashlight at the breezeway between the living room and kitchen and pushed the button a couple of times.

"What the hell are you up to, boy?" Mart said, talking more to himself than me as he picked his way cautiously through the kitchen. "If I bark my shin on something-."

I waited until I saw his silhouette move into the entryway. Closing my eyes and holding my breath, I pushed the plug into the socket. I heard a small snap as the current flooded down the wire and I sensed rather than saw a dim shimmer of light beyond my eyelids. I opened my eyes and looked.

The tree, looking far more full and perfect than it ever had any right to, towered in the corner of the room. It seemed to be floating above the ground, suspended within the warm pillow of pastel light emanating from the red and green glowing bulbs and the multicolored glassine reflections of twenty-two delicate, sun faded ornaments. Hundreds of long, mirrored slivers of tinsel shimmered on the hint of a breeze as the intricately crafted angel at the peak of the tree beckoned all to come closer, to bask in the symbolic luminescence of peace and goodwill both past and present.

It was the most beautiful Christmas tree I had ever seen in my life.

Mart didn't say a word. I knew he hadn't left the room, I could see his immobile shape still standing there, but he wasn't coming any closer, either.

I was suddenly sure I'd made a huge mistake.

"Merry Christmas," I tried, hoping I was wrong.

The seconds dragged by and still Mart was silent. The butterflies fluttering around inside my guts all died at once and fell to form a black, greasy ball of dread that rode heavy in the pit of my stomach.

Knowing I was going to have to face the consequences eventually, I started to reach for the lamp next to the sofa.

"Leave it off, would you, son?" Mart's voice was quiet and neutral.

Pulling my arm back, I slowly straightened up and waited for whatever was coming.

Mart stood there a while longer before slowly making his way across the room to stand in the glow of the tree, staring at it. My heart sank in my chest as I saw his tears.

"It took the weeds a good year to swallow up that

tree," he said softly. "I kept telling myself to get out there and collect her decorations before it was too late, but I just couldn't bring myself to do it, there were too many memories of her... of the kids."

The old man's voice trailed away as he reached up to touch one of the smaller, less ornate bulbs.

"Then one day it was too late," he lamented. "There was a storm... a hail storm. I ran for the door as soon as I heard the ice bouncing off the roof but I knew it was too late the second I stepped outside. I knew how delicate Mary's ornaments were and I knew there was no way any of them could have survived that hail. I just stood there on the porch and watched until it was done and then I went back inside. All I could do after that was pray that Mary understood somehow, that she could make some sense out of why I hadn't cherished the only material things in this world that she had truly loved, when I couldn't even understand it myself."

Still staring at the tree, Mart pulled out his ever-present handkerchief to wipe his eyes and blow his nose.

"Thank you, son," he said, looking at me as he tucked the handkerchief away. "This means more to me than you will ever know. Merry Christmas."

I smiled, never suspecting that one day this moment in time would mean as much to me as it did to him.

"Merry Christmas," I said.

I found Mart sleeping in his chair when I went into the house that night. He was fine. He told me he hadn't been sleeping very well lately and must have nodded off while reading the paper before it got dark. He claimed the phone never rang- said he would have heard it if it had.

Maybe Mart did sleep through the ringing of the phone less than a foot from his ear. Maybe, and this would be a far more reasonable, the operator dialed the wrong number. I didn't know and I didn't care. Real or imagined, I knew how close I'd come to losing my chance and I wasn't going to let this one go.

Two days later- two glorious days of the two of us talking and laughing and reminiscing- Mart died in his chair while we were watching the evening news on TV.

"Can you believe these guys?" I asked as we watched a clip of the Lions game... and Mart didn't answer. One minute he was there, the next he was gone.

Junior Baker, a gregarious, dry-witted man who happened to own the next farm over from Mart's, stopped by the house a couple days later while I was getting dressed for Mart's visitation service. Junior's real first name was actually Charles, the same as his father's, a man who had been one of Mart's closest friends until he died in a farming accident in '58, but I'd never heard anyone call him anything other than Junior, a name that certainly belied both the man's physical stature and the respect folks had for him. He was one of those rare people I actually liked without reservation from the first time I met him.

Besides following in the farming footsteps of his father, Junior was also a deacon on the board of Mart's church. When I saw his car pulling up to the house I naturally assumed he was just stopping by to extend his and the church's condolences, but it turned out I was wrong. While Junior did extend his and the church's condolences, that wasn't the only reason he'd dropped by. Junior Baker was also the executor of Mart's estate, and as executor, he had stopped in to give me an envelope that Mart had left for me. He also told me I had been named in Mart's will, the reading of which was scheduled for the day after Mart's funeral, but that wasn't important to me at the time. The important thing to me was whatever message Mart had left for me inside the envelope.

I didn't open it until later that night. I couldn't bring myself to do it before then. Mart had only been gone for two days, I was still reeling at the edge of the vast insurmountable chasm that separates the living from the dead, still trying to comprehend the enormity of the gulf, still awed by the sudden finality of it all. Mart was dead. He wasn't lost, he wasn't hiding, he wasn't going to call; he was dead. He had ceased to be...except for the contents of that envelope. While I knew it was only a temporary reprieve, in some small way I felt he wouldn't truly be gone until I opened it and I didn't want to let him go.

There were two items in the envelope, a letter and one half of a tattered hundred-dollar bill.

I guess he thought it made more sense than taking it with him to his grave.

Ken,

If you are reading this then that means I must be laid out up to Maxwell's Funeral Parlor waiting on my last ride to the cemetery.

I imagine you are probably feeling pretty low right now. I know how you feel, boy, I've lost more loved ones than I care to count. Go ahead and grieve if you have to, just don't let it get away from you. Remember son, that's not me in that casket, that's just the husk I used to live in. You know where I am.

Unless I miss my guess, Junior Baker just left and you are probably sitting at the kitchen table reading this, maybe sitting in the same chair I'm sitting in right now. I like that. It seems right to me.

It's a wonderful place, this house. It's seen a lot of births and deaths and everything in between. It's been a fine home that's always known a lot of love and I know nothing would make my daddy happier than to see it go to you, so that's the way it's going to be. I'm leaving you the house and the ten-acre chunk of land it sits on, everything else goes to the church. You'll hear about it as soon as the lawyer gets around to reading my will but I thought it might be better if you heard it from me first.

You remind me a lot of my father, son, you always have. You were both born with a rough row to hoe but neither of you ever let it get the best of you. You've inspired me to be a better man and for that, I thank you.

I'm damned proud to have known you Ken Malone and you can be sure I will be telling your mother the same as soon as I see her.

Martin

I slipped Mart's half of our bill into the pocket of his suit coat just before the funeral director closed his casket for the last time.

"I'll see you when I see you," I whispered.

I kept my end of my bargain with God.

Now, I can't actually say God came down and told me straight out that he wanted me to be an eighth grade English teacher, but I can tell you I was remembering my open ended promise to him when I made the choice to switch my major from electrical engineering to straight education.

Oh, I can hear your argument. You just let your imagination get carried away that night, dad, you took Mart's not answering the phone and blew it all out of proportion. You could have offered to give up Oreo Cookies and Mart would still have been alive when you got home that night. And maybe you're right...but a promise is a promise and I've never regretted the decision for even a minute.

The girl who would one day be your mom and I had two classes together when school started up again in the fall of '79, social sciences 201 and English 102 (creative writing), and let me tell you, son, I lived for those two classes that semester. I was enamored with her from the first day of class and I did everything I could to get her to notice me. I always wore my best pair of jeans and a clean looking shirt to class. I washed, conditioned, and blow dried my David Cass- er , uh...Steven Tyler hair until it looked just so, and, after overhearing her tell another girl she enjoyed soft rock from the sixties, I started whistling songs in the hall on the way to class, songs like Traces by the Classic Four and Cherish by the Association.

I got nothing. Oh, she was polite and friendly, she always smiled when I held the door open for her and she never made any disgusted gagging type gestures on the few occasions our eyes accidentally met across the room, but she never really noticed me either... until I made her cry.

Dr. Holton, our instructor for creative writing, would occasionally pick out different students to read one of their classmate's writing assignments from the day before. The object of this exercise was to get a discussion going amongst the students about whether or not the writer (who wasn't required to claim ownership of the piece) had accomplished what he or she had set out to do, and if not, why. Aspiring writers as a whole are a notoriously critical bunch and this class was definitely not the exception that proved the rule; this was no holds barred and no feelings were spared. It was a tough crowd.

One day Dr. Holton gave us a list of six or seven descriptive topics- a winding dirt road, a dying tree, an old toy, etc- and told us to write a story in a thousand words or less based on the topic of our choice. The topic I chose was the last on the list, a worn record, and, fittingly enough, the title I gave the story I wrote was The Worn Record.

A couple days later, after Dr. Holton had read and graded the assignment, several of the stories were handed out to different students to be read aloud in front of the class. One of those students was your mom and, although I didn't know it until she read the title out loud, the story she had been given to read was mine.

I was scared to death. Not only was the class about to hear and pronounce judgment on a nakedly emotional type story, a story which was likely to be accredited to a girl, or possibly the gay guy sitting a couple chairs over from me, Diane Wilson, the object of my unrequited affection, was standing up at the podium with my story in her hands; she could see my name on the paper, she knew I was responsible for what she was about to read!

I was a wreck. I leaned over my table, held my head in my hands, and kept my eyes closed. I tried to monitor the class's reaction by listening for uninterested paper shuffling, whispered comments, and- worse by far- sarcastic yawns, but the only thing I could hear over the adrenalin charged pounding of my anxious heart was your mom's voice. I held my breath until she was done (roughly three and a half minutes) and then I held it some more while I waited for a reaction.

The story worked! Your mother's voice trembled almost imperceptibly as she read the last line, there was a momentary pause of silence, and then I received the highest praise possible from a group of aspiring authors... a short smattering of applause from roughly a third of the class. Astounded and relieved, I took a breath and looked up at the sound of their clapping, but promptly forgot about everyone else in the room except for the girl staring at me from the podium, the beautiful girl with tears in her sparkling brown eyes.

We were married on June third, 1982, the happiest day of our lives... until we had you.

But wait...

I hid my old battered suitcase away in a crawlspace one rainy day in 1975. If Mart had seen me do it, or if one of my friends had stumbled across it somehow after I did it, I would have told them I was just storing it there, keeping it out of the way until I needed it... which, now that I think about it, wouldn't have been a lie.

I didn't hide that suitcase out of shame, I wasn't embarrassed by the way it looked or of the things it held, but I can't honestly say I was proud of them either. My feelings for that suitcase and its contents lay somewhere beyond being proud or ashamed, my feelings ran much deeper than that, out there in the unexplainable realm of death and love and dreams, of miracles and crushing disappointment, of hope and despair. I couldn't talk to anyone about those things, I couldn't cheapen the heartache and miracles by saying something like, 'Oh that's just some stuff from when I was a kid', nor could I ever hope to fully explain them, it just wasn't possible. So I hid them away.

The crawlspace was (and still is) behind a loose board in the back of the closet in my bedroom upstairs- the same bedroom Mart and his brothers had when they were boys, Mart's sons had after him and, unless you and your mom have moved, the same bedroom you have now. The suitcase is still there as I write this, still hidden away after all these years, still holding the only evidence of a time in my life that I have always kept hidden away in my heart; a faded stub of a Greyhound bus ticket, a bunch of books stolen from a library out in California, half of a tattered hundred-dollar bill, and a letter from an old man.

I thought about taking that suitcase out and giving it to your mom to hang on to for you but I've decided I like the idea of leaving it right where it is. Maybe you'll have already found that battered suitcase before you read this. Maybe you've already made those things your own and puzzled over how they came to be there. Maybe you've separated them and hid the ticket stub and the ragged half of that hundred-dollar bill away in your own secret spot to take out and show a friend of yours when his mom drops him off to spend the night, maybe you've read some of the books and wondered why one of them, a western by Louis L'Amour, is missing a couple of pages. Maybe you've taken the letter to your mom and asked her who Ken and Mart were. Or maybe you haven't. Either way, those things belong to you now. I want you to have them.

I drove out to California during summer break of 1981 to find my dad. Your mom and I were already engaged and I was hoping, if I could find him, to invite him to the wedding. I was hoping for a lot of things, actually, but that was the reason I gave your mom for my going.

I found his grave in a sprawling and neglected city owned cemetery located in one of the seedier sections of Venice. My dad had died on the floor of a bathroom in a back street bar in 1978. Two men in the bar had been arguing, one pulled a gun, took a shot at the other and missed. The bullet went through the wall at the other end of the bar and hit my dad in the head as he was standing at the urinal. He was dead before he hit the floor. The guy that fired the shot pleaded guilty to a reduced charge of involuntary manslaughter and a firearm violation and was sentenced to five years in jail.

Cindy was the only member of my family to attend our wedding - or at least the only living member. Jim was just an unpleasant memory by this time, they'd gotten divorced in 1977, but the guy she brought with her to the wedding (and would eventually end up marrying) didn't look like any prize either.

They both died two years later when their car veered off the road and slammed into a tree. The police were never able to determine who was behind the wheel but both bodies were found to have had a blood alcohol level of twice the legal limit.

Thursday June 14, 1995 *The Trufant Citizen*

Builders Unearth Human Remains

(Spencer Township) *Eric Carlsen's construction crew had just finished setting forms for the basement walls of a new home site in Spencer Township when he noticed an oddly familiar looking rock jutting from wall of the freshly dug hole.*

"My first thought when I noticed it was, 'Hey, that rock looks kinda' like a skull,' said Carlsen, the foreman of the crew, "but I honestly didn't really believe it was a skull until I pulled it out of the dirt and saw those two empty eye sockets looking back up at me."

"It really shook him up," said Denny Gosen, owner of Integrity Construction in Greenville and Carlsens' employer. "The whole crew was still lookin' a little green around the gills when I got here an hour or so later."

The skeletal remains found on Tuesday apparently are those of an adolescent, but Kent County sheriff's investigators say the site is not a crime scene, or at least not a modern one.

"The skull shows no sign of any dental work and is obviously very old," said Kent County Sheriff's Deputy Geoff LaRue, "but I would still have to label the death as suspicious. The gravesite was very shallow, the remains were found to be in an unnatural position for a proper burial, and several older, cork type bottles and other artifacts were found in the soil directly beneath the body."

The remains were found in sandy soil at the home sight on Stanton Road, about seven miles west of Trufant. Workers say a dilapidated log building was removed from the sight last year in preparation for the new construction.

The dilapidated log building referred to in this newspaper clipping was the lilac hidden cabin Mart and I visited the day he gave me the fifty-cent tour. There was never any doubt in my mind that the remains were of Mart's best friend, David Johansson.

The bones were sent to Michigan State University and eventually identified as the remains of a young, Caucasian male of approximately 10 to 16 years of age. The cause of death was never determined but they were able to estimate he had been dead for about a hundred years before he was found. Based on the artifacts recovered from beneath the body, they believed the boy's grave was actually the bottom of an old outhouse hole.

I contacted the state police as soon as I heard about the body and told them what Mart had told me about the circumstances leading up to David's disappearance in 1905. I also asked that I be allowed to claim the remains when MSU finished their examination. They thanked me for the information and told me they'd get back to me.

I did some research while I waited for MSU to finish and I found there was one unused plot left in the Sand Lake Cemetery and it happened to be fairly close to Mart's grave. It had been one of two plots purchased by a man named Stephen Crandall in 1932, one for himself and one for his wife. According to Junior Baker, who by this time was one of the oldest residents in the area, Mrs. Crandall had run off with a Fuller Brush man one fine spring day in 1940 and Mr. Crandell, after reading the letter his wife had left for him, immediately set about putting his plot to good use by running a hot load of buckshot through his brain. Since Mrs. Crandell had never come back to claim her plot, I contacted the township board, explained what I wanted to do and, with some prodding from Junior, the township agreed to donate the plot. Your mother and I provided the headstone.

David Johansson was finally laid to rest on June first, 1996. It was a beautiful sunny day and forty-four people were present at the graveside service for a boy none of us had ever known.

We found out your mother was pregnant with you in June of 2000, eighteen years almost to the day after we were married.

Your mom and I had all but given up on ever having any children. There wasn't any explanation for it, we'd both been checked out and there weren't any physical problems to prevent us from conceiving a child, but it just wasn't happening. There were options of course, we could have visited a fertility clinic or your mom could have taken one of a variety of drugs, but we both felt since there was absolutely no reason for us not to be able to do it on our own, maybe it would be best if we left well enough alone and let God decide whether we were fit to be parents or not.

We didn't tell anyone about you at first, at least not verbally, but I think a few of the other teachers we worked with may have suspected after watching us walking on air in the hallways at school and making goo-goo eyes at each other in the teachers' lounge over lunch for the five months that passed before we felt confident enough to let the cat out of the bag. Oh, and I finally quit smoking for good, something your mom had been after me to do since our first date, and I'm sure that raised some eyebrows.

I couldn't smoke in school of course (those glorious days of polluting the teachers' lounge had petered out and died right along with the vinyl record album and Ma Bell back in 1986), but I smoked on the drive in, I took a drive every day during lunch, and I had one going for the drive home just as soon as the front wheels of my car were across the school's property line, and most, if not all of the other teachers were contemptuously aware of it.

I had made several half hearted attempts to quit before finding out that you were on the way but the time never seemed to be right. I couldn't quit during the school year because I'd snap at the kids, I couldn't quit during the first eight weeks of summer break because I taught driver's training- a job more inclined to make me smoke more rather than less- and I certainly couldn't quit during the last four weeks of summer break because that was the only time of the year that I had to kick back and relax and work around the house. How could I relax if I couldn't smoke? Excuses? Man, I had a million of them, but it all came down to the plain and simple fact that I just didn't want to quit... that and I didn't like the idea of people telling me I had to quit. Questioning authority, it seemed, was something I never grew out of. But then I found out about you and Boom, just like that, I was done with cigarettes. It wasn't easy but it certainly didn't kill me.

I was going to be a good father, a great father. I had been practicing on other people's kids for years, teaching them, learning from them, trying to help those that needed help when they would let me, and I had come to look at my experience in the classroom as kind of a prep class, a kind of Algebra 2 for parenthood, if you will. While I didn't think I needed a prep class on parenthood – I was sure I knew enough to be a father at twenty-two and I almost certainly would have ignored God's advise to wait if he'd left it up to me to decide – that decision wasn't mine to make. Now that you were on the way, it all made perfect sense to me... for a while.

Your mom and I made a lot of preparations for your arrival. We bought baby things- clothes, toys, a bassinette, a stroller; you name it, if we thought you needed it we bought it. We baby-proofed the drawers and the cabinets, we cleaned the house from top to bottom, shampooed the rugs, installed new smoke and carbon monoxide detectors, painted the upstairs bedroom that would eventually be yours a light shade of blue... and I decided to double the amount of my life insurance policy.

"No problem," my agent said when I told him. "All we'll need before we make the change is a clean bill of health from your doctor. When was the last time you had a complete physical?"

"Ten years ago?" I guessed.

"No good," he said. "Has to have been within the last two. Why don't you go ahead and get one scheduled and get back to me after you get a clean bill of health, okay?"

I went ahead and made an appointment with my doctor for the following week and I kept it. Six days after my physical- four months before you were born- the tests were confirmed and I was told I had something called Stage Four Adenocarcinoma of the Lung... advanced lung cancer.

The doctor advised me that I had about six months to live if I elected to undergo chemotherapy or two to three without.

I took the chemo.

You are a quiet baby. You seldom cry and when you do, it's never for more than a minute or two. Your hair is blond and fine. The grip of your tiny fist around my finger is firm and strong. Sometimes when I'm holding you in my arms, you stare at me and I think I see the weight of the world looming in those precious eyes; you look so sad and helpless, so scared. I worry when I see that look.

I think you know.

I tell myself I'm being silly- I've read the books, watched the tapes, I know it's impossible for you to be aware of anything beyond those things that you can see, feel, and touch, I know you have no cognoscente reasoning, no sense of self or time. But still, I think you know.

I have so many things I want to tell you, so many things to show you, so many things to experience with you. I want to watch you grow. I want you to reach up and take my hand when you're frightened and I want to feel the pang of regret that will eventually come when you don't. I want to introduce you to people as my son, watch while you shake their hand and feel proud when they compliment you on your manners. I want to look at you someday and wonder how you got to be so big, so mature, so self-reliant. I want to grow old and talk to you about the life you've made for yourself.

I'm trapped. I can see you. I can touch you, talk to you, hold you, but I can't stay with you. I can see the promise of your life but only though the insurmountable crosshatch of cancer and time. I've done all I can, I've searched for a way to escape this fate and I've fought as hard as I could, but it's too late; the doors of my past have closed behind me and I can't go back.

I don't know how old you are as you read this, nor do I know why your mother decided the time was right to give you this monstrosity that started off as a simple letter from a father to his son, but I'm guessing you are probably fourteen, that sometimes terrible age between childhood and the destiny that you have just begun to suspect is yours to chose, and I imagine you've been getting into some kind of trouble at home or school or maybe even with the police. I think you're probably angry, not so much at one particular thing but at everything. I know that anger, son; I felt it too.

You live in a strange world, David, a frantic, crowded world, an impatient world ruled by tiny cell phones and satellites and computers and greed. A world that demands participation while discouraging self-examination, a world where it is far easier for a man to control his universe than it is to control himself. A world that promises happiness, dangles it out in front of you like a carrot on a string, but never delivers. Want to be fulfilled? Buy a new car. Reassured? Buy a bigger house. Confident? Pick a surgeon. Happy? Oh, that'll come eventually... have you tried a vacation in the Caymans?

Don't waste your life searching the world for happiness, son, you'll never find it. Look to yourself, appreciate what you have while you've got the chance- you'll never be happy later if you can't find a reason to be happy now. Know yourself and know your God. Listen to your heart and make a choice.

Don't be in a hurry to grow up, enjoy being young while you've got the chance, you'll never get another. Try to look at it as a prep class for being an adult. You can skip ahead if you want to, you can keep your anger alive, feed it, nurse it, wear it on your sleeve and surround yourself with friends that feel the same, but being an adult never ends and you'll always regret the time you gave up.

Appreciate the time you have with your mom, she's a strong woman who you can learn a lot from and she deserves your respect. Okay, so maybe she's a little strict and old fashioned (if your mom read this before giving it to you- and I told her she could- I'm guessing there's at least two words that have been censored from this text with a thick black marker), I won't argue with you there, but she's been through a lot and she knows more about life than you'll ever be able to comprehend until the shoe is on the other foot and you have a child or two of your own. Trust her judgment, son, both in your life and in hers, and do your best to support her decisions, she deserves to be happy. Go ahead and argue for a later curfew, just never forget that she loves you more than any other person on this planet. Treat her like she could be taken from you tomorrow.

I always knew you would be the one person I would talk to about those four timeless days in 1974 but I never imagined it would be like this. I had always pictured us walking in the woods together or maybe camping or fishing on a quiet, desolate lake where my words could be backlit with the sights and sounds of the miracles that most so easily take for granted... but now I have to wonder if this might not have been the only way you could have ever heard what it was that I so desperately wanted you to understand.

David Martin Malone. You were named after a boy who died too young and an old man who once thought he had lived too long. Without them, you never would have been born.

You have a purpose in life, David. No one can tell you what it is, that's something you're going to have to figure out on your own. And while I might not be there to help you, at least I was given a chance to tell you this; you've got a lot of folks pulling for you, boy. Keep your chin up and give 'er everything you've got.

I love you, son. I always will.

I promise.

Dad

English 102
Ken Malone
Dr. Holton

The Worn Record

The man looked down into his wife's eyes as they danced. His wife. Even now, after three years of marriage, that phrase still filled him with a heady mixture of love and pride.

"Any regrets, Mr. Thomas?" she asked, tilting her head coyly.

"None, Mrs. Thomas," he replied, giving her a gentle kiss. "You're just as beautiful as..."

The old man woke with a start and sat up in his chair trying to get his bearings. His wife's respirator softly hummed. The old clock on the nightstand clicked. He picked up his cane, the handle worn smooth from years of use, and made his way over to the edge of his wife's bed and looked down on her as she slept.

Two years ago the doctors had told him she would be gone in six months, yet she lived, unwilling or unable to surrender her life to the cancer within her.

She had been this way for three months, the first two in the hospital until he had been able to convince the doctors he could care for her in their home. "It won't make any difference to her," they told him. "She'll never know if she's here or there." But he knew they were wrong and he persisted.

Now, four weeks later, he had to admit the doctors had known the truth. There had been no change and he was getting very tired.

As he gazed at her face, he realized how old and frail she had become. When did this happen, he wondered. Just yesterday they had gotten married. He could remember every little detail, every person who had attended. He remembered how beautiful she had been when he lifted the veil up onto her hair so he could kiss her, the way her eyes had sparkled with tears and her lower lip had trembled as they kissed for the first time as husband and wife.

He quickly turned his head from his wife, fighting back tears of despair and helplessness.

As he gained control he found himself looking at the old Victrola standing against the wall. It had been there since the day he brought it home as a birthday present for her. He had saved every spare cent he could for nearly a year, hoping fervently that there would be enough money in time for her birthday, and he had made it with six days to spare. He even had enough to buy a record so they could play it the night he brought it home.

And play it they had. The same song, over and over again, never tiring of it. "Let's listen to it again," she would plead each time it ended. "All right," he'd reply, smiling and rolling his eyes. "But this is the last time." Then he would wind the crank, secretly hoping she would want to listen to it just once more after it finished.

The old man slowly stood, walked over to the Victrola and ran his hand over its varnished lid. He tried to recall the last time it had been played but the memory was gone. Cautiously he lowered himself down onto one knee, his face contorted with the effort and the pain of arthritis. He opened the front of the cabinet, reached inside and pulled out the thirty or so records that had been stored there. Placing them on the floor, he slowly began to sort through the titles, stopping with each one to smile at the memories of the times it had been played.

The smile trailed away from his face as he came to the last record in the stack. This was it. This was the record he had brought home with the Victrola that first night.

The old man pushed himself up from the floor and gently placed the record on his bed. Opening the lid of the

Victrola, he picked out the crank from inside and fitted it into the slot on the side of the machine. The voice of the salesman came floating back. "Now just turn this crank twenty-five times and release this lever right here. That's all there is to it. She'll play the whole thing without slowing down a lick."

As he turned the crank, the springs inside squeaked from years of disuse and lack of oil. He stopped after twenty turns; his aching arm would not allow him to turn it any further. He placed the record on the turntable and released the lever. As he lowered the arm, he picked up his cane from where it leaned against the wall. The needle scratched faintly as it moved along the groove while he made his way to his wife's bed.

Just as he placed his hand on his wife's, the first strains of the song came drifting from the Victrola. The melody played and the man looked to his wife, remembering that night so long ago when they had giggled and danced to this music. As he gazed at her a tear welled up in her eye and slowly began to trace the wrinkles of her face as it traveled down her cheek.

"I love you," the man whispered.

And the music played on.

Acknowledgements

Regrets and Promises is just a small harvest of a few of the countless seeds of hope and love sowed over many generations by various members of my family. While many of these individuals are still here on this earth to thank in person, I would like to take this opportunity to acknowledge my everlasting gratitude to a few of those who are not:

My great grandmothers, Nellie Webster Brown and Lena Betts Carmien, two farmwives who, though they never met, lived oddly parallel lives of pain, hardship, and sacrifice in raising 7 babies apiece during the Great Depression. They both lived harder lives than anyone living today can even begin to imagine and they did it on their own. I am in awe of these two ladies.

My maternal grandparents, Martin and Beulah Brown, for their love and their unwavering determination in giving their children a better life than either of them had ever known.

My paternal grandmother, Edrie Carmein McGarry, for never giving up on looking for the best in life.

My aunt, Shirley McGarry Barnard, for being there for her kid brother when he needed her.

I would also like to thank:

Walter Barnard, for the unconditional patience, understanding, and guidance he offered so selflessly some fifty years ago.

My parents, Mitchell and Charlotte McGarry, for their lifetime of personal discipline in always trying to do what was best for their two boys and for never giving up on either of us, no matter what we put them through.

My mother and father-in-law, Larry and Loretta Lind, for the quiet help and support they have always been so graciously ready to give.

Walter Lockwood, for the thousands of unpaid hours he so freely gave over the years to help his students. May your retirement be long, fulfilling, and aspiring-writer free... you have certainly earned it. Thank you, sir.

Jeff Streelman, Nancy Magnus, and Kim Whitley, for giving far more of themselves for this novel than they could ever reasonably hope to receive in return.

And finally, I would like to thank my wife, Stacy, for always being there. From lover and best friend to nurse and confidant, you have been and always will be, everything to me.

I love you, hon.